DOCTOR SALT

DOCTOR SALT

Gerard Donovan

Scribner

First published in Great Britain by Scribner, 2005
An imprint of Simon & Schuster UK Ltd
A Viacom Company

Scribner and design are trademarks of Macmillan Library Reference USA,
Inc., used under licence by Simon & Schuster, the publisher of this work.

1 3 5 7 9 10 8 6 4 2

Simon & Schuster UK Ltd
Africa House
64–78 Kingsway
London WC2B 6AH

www.simonsays.co.uk

Simon & Schuster Australia
Sydney

A CIP catalogue record for this book is available from the British Library

Hardback ISBN 0-7432-6358-8
EAN 9780743263580
Trade Paperback ISBN 0-7432-6852-0
EAN 9780743268523

Typeset by M Rules
Printed and bound in Great Britain by
Mackays of Chatham plc

for Giles, David and Hobart

And so for ever, brother, hail and farewell

CATULLUS

Sunless

SUNLESS 1

Sunless went to visit a doctor once.

He waited in the reception hall until his name was called, and then he walked along a burgundy rug to the doctor's suite, such a famous doctor that he didn't have the title 'Doctor' before his name on the door, just 'Mr Fargoon'. His surgery didn't look like a doctor's office: the light was low and soft, and bookcases lined the walls. A mild green plant reached to the window from a polished oak desk. Mr Fargoon wore a white linen suit and a blue tie, and he did not look up as Sunless walked to the chair in front of the desk. Behind Fargoon, Sunless saw a drawing of a fish on the wall. No sea, no angler, no sky. Just a fish. It didn't even say what type.

'Mr Sunless, please sit.' Fargoon showed him the armchair and opened his file.

Sunless said, 'It's actually *Sunless*. No *Mister*.'

'Noted.' Fargoon crossed something out and continued not to look at him.

'We have an hour or thereabouts, Sunless, and much to discuss.'

'I see.'

'Why do you think you're here?' Fargoon said.

'I don't know, not this time anyway.'

'Then just talk about yourself.'

Sunless pointed with his eyes: 'Why is there no sea around the fish?'

'What?' Fargoon turned to it and lifted an eyebrow. 'No, no, let's begin. We have only so much time, you understand.'

'I understand.'

Fargoon looked at his patient's chin. 'Your condition, Sunless.'

Sunless talked for maybe an hour or a bit more. Fargoon said nothing but wrote a lot, turning pages silently. After Sunless finished, Fargoon still said nothing. Then he tore a scrap of paper off the end of the page and wrote something. He handed it to his patient.

'That's what's wrong with you,' he said.

Sunless read two words.

'That's my diagnosis,' Fargoon said. 'And now I will read to you a summary of what those two words mean.'

He reached behind him and took a book from the shelves, then coughed.

'Paranoia, auditory hallucinations, extreme agitation, heightened awareness, an extreme coldness to others, with the added category of delusion of persecution.'

He wrote a prescription. 'Try this. It's very new, very promising. They'll fill it down the hall.'

Sunless got up to leave Fargoon's office.

But before he left, Sunless did say something to him. He said, 'I have my own definition.'

'Really,' Fargoon said, writing in his notebook.

'I do.'

'Well, let's hear it.' Fargoon closed his book, put his fingers under his chin, and looked at his patient's chest.

SUNLESS 2

Sunless, now that's a name. Sunless liked to leave it at that. He didn't have a second name because one sufficed, and anyway he believed what was wrong with him didn't have a name, or had many, which amounted to the same thing. One name could do for just about anything, Sunless thought.

That visit to Fargoon was not his first.

No, Sunless had been to Fargoon's office a month or so before that, though on that occasion Fargoon was delayed and Sunless had to wait in the main hallway where other people waited outside other doctors' offices. He sat on a chair, one of a line of chairs.

The television on the white wall opposite him broadcast the RX-24 health channel, owned by Pharmalak, the same outfit that owned the hospital Fargoon worked at. It was hard for Sunless not to watch and listen because he sat on his own and everyone was too far away to hear them talking. The screen changed to a shot of a man with a furrowed brow sitting beside a window beyond which children played on a swing. A woman's voice sounded over the picture of the man:

'Are you tired all day? Experiencing mood swings? Find yourself irritable at children, noise, social situations? Do you frequently wish you could be alone? If you have experienced one or more of these symptoms over the past few weeks, you may be suffering from Aggravated Sensitivity Disorder, or ASD. Talk to your doctor. On your screen is a list of participating doctors. If you wish, you can test a product developed to alleviate these symptoms. Contact Pharmalak and you will receive a sample approximately four days before your first appointment.

'And in the news: another storm has hit the Salt Lake Valley, causing damage to hundreds of homes. The police have advised homeowners to monitor the situation as the cleanup begins.

'This news may cause anxiety, but do you find that you're never content at holidays and special social events? Feeling left out of the party? Inevitably disappointed? Perhaps your expectations have not been met, or you feel isolated and burdened with anticipation? You may be suffering from Seasonal Anxiety Disorder, or SAD. A product has been developed that may alleviate the effects of this disorder. Talk to your doctor. On your screen is a list of participating doctors. If you wish—'

'Mr Sunless?'

'Yes,' Sunless said to the wall.

'Mr Fargoon will see you now.' The screen door behind him slid shut.

Sunless entered Fargoon's office. Inside, Fargoon smiled him to a seat, where Sunless sat and described how he felt. Fargoon listened to his patient for about an hour, listed the effects Sunless described of the previous medication, and then wrote down what was wrong with him.

Fargoon wrote three words.

This time, Fargoon explained to Sunless that he had a chronic form of Borderline Depersonalization Disorder. He explained what it was, gave Sunless a prescription, 'still in trials,' he said, but extremely effective, he said, 'in over sixty percent of cases of the same symptoms where other medications had failed completely'.

As he handed Sunless the script, Fargoon shook his head.

'Finding out what's wrong with a person,' he said, 'is like swinging a hammer in the dark. Sometimes I get it first time, *bang*, one prescription, and other times,' he pursed his lips, 'a few months, a few years.' He rested his chin on his hand. 'It can even take a lifetime. Are you ready for that, Sunless?'

'Am I ready for a lifetime?'

'To find out what's wrong with you.'

Sunless laughed. 'As long as I get some life left over, once you do find out.'

'Life left over?

'To live for a while.'

Fargoon rose and smiled over his patient's shoulder. 'That may be hoping for too much.' He raised an arm to the door. 'You may have to learn to live with it.'

Sunless said, 'I don't have to learn – I'm doing that anyway.'

Fargoon held his signalling position. He smiled. 'I will see you soon, Sunless.'

Down the hall, Sunless showed his prescription to the nurse. She handed him a bottle of yellow pills.

'Good, Sunless,' she said. 'Here you are. That's a month's worth. You're all ready to go.'

'Ever notice,' he said.

She smiled. 'What?'

'That *pill* is *ill* with a "p"?'

'Never thought of that. They do sound the same.'

'I mean the spelling.'

'That's what I meant.'

Putting the pills in his pocket, Sunless waited in the common room, located to the right of the reception hall, until the other patients joined him. They could see the tracks from the window, and a bell sounded when the train arrived to take him back to his house. At that point Sunless remembered that he had forgotten to ask Fargoon a question he had travelled the best part of an hour on the train to ask:

'Where did you put my father and what did you do with him?'

That was a fairly important question, he thought. And I forgot.

Two posters flanked the door. The first showed a child with her head bowed as a kitten looked on, and underneath that Sunless read:

'Is your child constantly sad? It could be depression or even bipolar disease, a serious medical condition. Talk to your doctor about Elevax.'

The second showed an old man standing in a doorway and scratching his head as if he couldn't find something.

'Have you talked to your doctor lately? It might be time to discuss Nemocot.'

If Sunless were an honest man he would admit that the session before was also not the first time he had visited Fargoon. He had seen the doctor for many months. His life was a large file in Fargoon's office, and Fargoon had a lot of files. So many patients, no wonder Fargoon never looked directly at him. What was the point? Another voice bleating out his troubles.

But once, and once only, Sunless managed to make Fargoon look up at him. Got him to stop writing and look. It was the day he told Fargoon about the October flies.

They had talked as usual, meaning Sunless had talked as usual. After he detailed for the doctor how he had reacted to the previous medication, Sunless spoke the next sentence deliberately, leaving plenty of space between the words so that Fargoon would catch up and match his writing to each word:

'I don't let flies live in my house after September.'

Fargoon simply continued to write, since he never said anything while Sunless spoke.

Sunless said, 'Again, no flies after September. You won't find any. "And why not," I hear you say.' He waited for a response. Ten, fifteen seconds. Fargoon's pen ran out of words and waited for Sunless to say something. Outside the window, Sunless observed the mountain, green under a blue sky.

He spoke first.

'Once I was working on my computer and I heard a fly behind me looking at my screen. I swiped at it and nearly came off the chair. I continued working until it flicked across in front of me. I grabbed the mouse and tried to clobber it, but the thing managed always to stay beyond my reach while it recorded the contents of the screen. I didn't realize what was going on till it was too late. The fly probably recorded every room in my house, every letter, copied and filed in those bytes of eyes. *Flies* and *files*. Same letters. Easily mixed up, those words.

'I chased it around the room and then around the house. It escaped through a window I had foolishly left open because of the heat. I ran out the front door and saw it swirling around the garbage bags. That was my final proof. And what did it see in my garbage? I know you want to know, Mr Fargoon.'

Fargoon seemed to be writing, though his pen moved in small circles, not flowing from left to right: maybe he wasn't writing at all. Sunless waited for an answer. Fargoon stopped − or stopped pretending to write − and waited too.

Sunless broke first again.

'Well it saw everything. Everything! That's why flies can't leave people's garbage alone. Flies always find garbage. All that information: eating habits. What you've read. How often you clean your house. What you watch when you think you are not being watched. News item − you are always being watched. And it got away. Whatever information that fly got from my computer is now out there. Being reviewed, analysed.

'I took precautions after that. I bought five bottles of fly spray and some tape and sealed the doorjambs and sprayed the air and the walls, emptying one bottle, keeping the air wet with it. When the flies dropped, I scooped up the dead ones from the windowsill in case any were faking it. Flies are professionals. They get their name from what they do, which is fly. And where do they fly away to? I don't know. Where do they sleep? I don't know. But I know what they fly with. They have cameras on their backs, transmitters; it all goes to a room somewhere. Not all flies have transmitters – for instance, April flies, May flies, June, July, August flies – yes, I'll concede that those are probably just real flies. September is a transition month, and most likely a few real insects are mixed in, holdouts from the summer. But once September ends and I see one of them past its season, I know what I'm dealing with.

'September flies are bad enough, not knowing their true nature, I mean, but if I see an October fly, I know I've been upgraded by the powers-that-be. Those are government flies. No reason for them to be alive otherwise.

'I saw an October fly recently. I sat back behind my desk and turned the monitor toward it. I waved at the fly. I had typed two words.

'I KNOW.

'I chased it for fifteen or twenty minutes. I got to every door and crack before it did. Kept it airborne to run the fuel cell down. I crushed it against the window, squashed its eyes with the edge of a saucer, placed it in an envelope, and mailed it back to the government. I wrote, "Here's some of your used equipment. Do I get a finder's fee?" They never replied.'

Fargoon lifted his face and stared at Sunless.

Sunless said, 'Did you get that?'

'I did,' Fargoon said.

'And the last bit, about not getting an answer from the government?'

'I have it.'

That was the only time Fargoon ever looked at Sunless in all the time they had talked. He seemed a bit dejected, Fargoon, as he handed Sunless a prescription and told him to take it down the hall. Not the usual breezy professional. That was also the only time Fargoon didn't tell Sunless what was wrong with him. Changed Fargoon's routine, Sunless had. That was good for him, to have his routine broken. *Yes*, Sunless thought, *I did him a favour by altering his way of thinking. The man will get better in the end, even if I don't.*

SUNLESS 3

It was Monday, December 21.

Sunless woke as the sun found a crack in the blanket draped over his bedroom window. He fixed the blanket to shut out the light completely and dressed slowly to make sure nothing had been hidden in his clothes while he slept, and before leaving the bedroom raised a mirror at the door and turned it as he scanned the living room in case anyone lay in wait. Then he scanned the kitchen. People gathered to eat and talk in kitchens, so naturally the government sends in flies to listen.

When it appeared safe to do so, he allowed himself to make coffee and drink it in the closet but wedged the door open to the living room so that he could watch the morning news on television without them seeing him.

'And now for local Salt Lake City news.'

He never turned the television off because noise concealed his movements and disguised his comings and goings. These were ordinary precautions, and following them gave him a sense of reasonable cheer. When he finished the coffee, he emerged from the closet and placed his sunglasses on his nose and then around each ear. Snow in the forecast, the man pointing his wand at clouds.

Ten o'clock. Time to go see Fargoon, to get the train to

Pharmalak Research Hospital. Time to sit in Fargoon's office and talk for an hour, and after that hour, it would then be time to look Fargoon in the eye and say, 'Where is my father?' Or something like that.

But now it was time for the usual precautions. Sunless did not want to follow a routine that could be recognized by those trained to spot such things: heaven knows how many winged creatures patrolled the street.

He showered in the bathroom, as it had been a few days now since he had washed himself. The procedure was simple enough: he always washed himself after he washed himself. In other words, he covered his body with soap, then washed the soap off, dried himself thoroughly, and then showered in plain water, after which he dried himself with a different towel (laundered in dye-free powder) and emerged a smell-free Sunless, an anonymous Sunless.

He had travelled to the facility for six months in the same small blue and white train, a sixteen-seater with huge windows and a driver behind a tinted partition. The train brought him from the station near his house on the shores of the Great Salt Lake to the hospital, hidden way up the mountains, in Park City. He had developed a method of getting on the train without calling attention to himself because he knew what neighbours do, and that is, watch neighbours. Sunless therefore continually developed ideas and blueprints for keeping out of sight. On the refrigerator, under a fish magnet, he had pinned a note to himself: 'See note.' The actual note was in the drawer with the knives and forks. 'I built a man once as an experiment. He has no eyes or mouth or mind right now, but he's standing

in my closet. But he won't be in the closet for long. I'll
take him out shortly because I want to use him as a double
when I leave the house so that people will think I'm at
home. I'll stand him by the window and tie him to strings
that go up and down off a battery and play loud music so
they'll think he's dancing and someone's here. The whole
neighbourhood will think I'm still here. That's what I
need to do before I leave the house: leave a dancing man
behind.'

He opened the door to a crack and watched for a few
minutes. Observing little activity, Sunless slipped out the
back way, padlocked the door, and moved along the alley to
the street behind his house, where the tracks were. The
thing about the train was that it made no sound as it glided
along the magnet strips on the tracks. But he preferred not
to wait in the open – too many eyeballs taking in his business. Consequently, he used his pocket mirror at the top of
the alley to watch for the train without exposing himself to
public view before dashing out at the last moment. He
wondered if the driver got tired of slamming on the brakes
when he ran in front of the train, but Sunless would not
change a boarding strategy that was clearly working. He
thought, *That's when you go down, when you think outside your
precautions.*

Every month Sunless sat with other people on the ride
to and from the hospital. After he first joined the train as a
regular himself, Sunless counted them down one by one as
they failed to arrive for the trip. A passenger disappeared
every month, and even with another empty seat staring at
the rest of them, no one on the train ever spoke about it.
When just one remained, a young woman, she and Sunless

briefly exchanged glances, which Sunless instantly regretted. Never saw her again. Obviously went the way of the others. And no one notices. No one says a thing.

So on the last trip Sunless wore vigilance like skin. Nothing happened, but this might be the trip where Sunless joined the ranks of the disappeared; maybe a UFO ship was standing by in the middle of the Great Salt Lake Desert, out in the old Wendover air force base a hundred miles west at the Nevada border, near the Bonneville Flats. One landed there ten years ago; at least that's what the rumours said. Okay, so probably twenty years ago, at least they saw lights in the area — that's what people said. Perhaps all these monthly interviews and medicines were meant to prepare them for the final stage. They were the chosen ones. Prepare to blast off. You are representing Planet Earth. There's always a final stage, Sunless thought, and someone vanished those people somewhere, because they didn't come back. They disappeared, that's what they did. People have a habit of disappearing if you don't keep an eye on them.

But that would not happen to him.

He was too careful about routines and had studied the art of remaining anonymous in various books, mostly mail-order publications, and concluded that remaining anonymous involved both being seen and not being seen. So on one day of the week he went to a bar downtown called The Ancient Mariner, where he laughed and talked with the patrons — wearing a wig over his hair and a pillow under his shirt, of course — but an ordinary man nonetheless with dance halls in his eyes and beer on his smile, visible enough that if he went missing, people might ask questions like, 'What became of so-and-so?'

And on all the other days, he lived an inch from the shadows.

Sunless saw the train in his mirror and ran out, waving his arms. The train stopped and he got on. As he expected, the driver gave him a hostile glance and had, in fact, stopped greeting him after the first couple of trips because Sunless never answered. Sunless distrusted people who seemed very interested in names, and he wasn't getting drawn into any circle. No cosy sharing. Yes, he needed to watch the driver, but not enough that it looked like anything more than ordinary natural suspicion. He selected a seat at the back and sank low and scanned the street out the window, then tapped the armrest. The screen flashed bright in front of him, the RX-24 health channel, showing a man looking intently at a computer monitor.

'Have you ever stared for what seems like hours into empty space? Do you experience reality as a series of randomly connected points, or lose your sense of self while pursuing those points of connection? Have your friends commented that you appear absent-minded? If you have experienced one or more of these symptoms consistently for more than three weeks, you may be suffering from a condition called Combined Internet Symptoms, or CIS. A product has been developed that may alleviate the effects of this disorder. Talk to your doctor. On your screen is a list of participating doctors. If you wish, you can test a product developed to alleviate these symptoms. Contact Pharmalak and we will arrange for you to receive a sample approximately four days before your first appointment.

'While the wait may cause you anxiety, do you sense other vacuums in your life? Do you find yourself attempting to connect your social and professional experiences in order to feel whole? Have your friends or family commented that you continually link random objects or experiences in conversations? If so, you may be suffering from Web-Reflex Disorder, or WRD. This condition is closely related to CIS, but can induce hallucinations in addition to the previous symptoms. A product has been developed that may alleviate the effects of this disorder. Talk to your doctor. On your screen is a list of participating doctors. If you wish, you can test a product developed to alleviate these symptoms. Contact Pharmalak and you will receive a sample approximately four days before your first appointment.'

Sunless looked around as the train moved through the city streets and climbed into the foothills of the Wasatch mountain range. With the city receding behind him, he felt better. Once they cleared the slope, it was thirty minutes east to the Kimball Junction checkpoint station at the entrance to the valley, and then another few minutes to Park City and the hospital, where on the second floor of the research facility, Mr Fargoon doubtless sat at his desk with his files, in which, Sunless knew, evidence lay of a man who had recently gone missing, a man he knew to be his father. Today Fargoon wasn't going to fob him off with a prescription. Sunless was going to ask some hard questions, find his dad, bring him home.

I came, I saw, I retrieved.

Just as he allowed himself to relax with that thought, the driver hit the brakes and stopped at the last station before the mountains. Sunless thrust out his arms to buffer himself from the seat in front.

The door of the train slid open and three teenage girls and a man walked in. The girls sat five rows ahead of Sunless. The man looked up and down the rows before coming to the back seat and sitting to his left. Sunless shook his head. *There's always one.* You sit in a big, empty restaurant and *the one* will walk down the aisles and sit beside you.

The train eased up into the canyon. Sunless glanced behind him to see the city in the valley and beyond it that giant blue in the west, the remnants of prehistoric Lake Bonneville that once covered most of Utah in shallow water. At least that's what they said. Maybe there was never a lake and the government created one, a giant mirror to signal outer space. We have citizens ready for you to take.

Nevertheless, he enjoyed how clean the city looked from here. The man who sat beside him, of course, could not take the silence:

'So what's happening around the nation today?' he said.

His question lingered in the limbo it deserved. Sunless watched the girls, who clenched themselves into a tight circle of whispers, then folded his arms and stared ahead. Never encourage *the one* if he sits beside you. Ignore him. The man answered his own question.

'Another flu, I hear. Something in New Orleans this week. They say hundreds may be sick.'

Sunless sighed and looked away, out the window. The train had begun to climb the mountain. Cars wound on the road that ran beside the track: some had ski racks on top and children making faces out the window, though Sunless couldn't figure out at whom.

'But that's not what I heard,' the man continued. 'I heard that the water reached the city from that storm flood, maybe a foot. I tell you, the world is changing. We are engaged in change.'

The train reached the top of the canyon and accelerated. Now they were in the mountains proper. Sunless had turned his head to the window at right angles, as far as the anatomy of his neck allowed. But some people were immune to hints.

'Yes, indeed, what I heard,' the man said, 'is that a flu strain crept along the Gulf and hit last week. The world is, indeed, changing.'

Sunless had heard it all before. The end of the world? Yes, heard of that one. Take your pick of disasters. An asteroid hurtling toward earth, nuclear weapons taking us back to the Stone Age, the break-up of the last great iceberg belt. The terrorists are coming. That's what they want you to think. How about *nothing* is happening. Just the government. *Them.* Keep the terrorists alive and kicking on every news programme, that's the way you get to do your government searches. What's happening? The government is happening. It starts with *Sir, what's that in your pocket?* It ends with *Sir, what's that in your mind?*

He realized he must have accidentally turned off the video screen when the train stopped at the last station and now touched it:

'And in New Orleans, a variant of the Gulf flu has sickened hundreds. Antibodies are currently being

administered. A limited quarantine is in effect in two
city hospitals until further notice.

'The news of a quarantine may cause you to ask
yourself if *you* have ever felt completely shut off from
everyone. Unable to empathize with those around
you? Feeling as though you were lost in a fog? Body
parts that seem too large or not to belong to you?
Or simply experiencing a sense of general but
persistent disconnection? You may be suffering from
Expanded Depersonalization Syndrome, or EDS. A
product has been developed that may alleviate the
effects of this disorder.

A photograph of the Pharmalak facility flashed on to
the screen, under which fifteen or twenty names scrolled,
all smiling heads: Doctor this, Doctor that. Sunless kept one
eye on the man beside him, who pulled a book and two
pamphlets from his briefcase and then turned to Sunless,
holding them up.

'I wonder if you'd be interested in looking at these,' the
man said. 'I happen to have some with me.'

Sunless pretended to listen to the news, but as luck
would have it, the screen went silent, simply showing a still
photograph of Pharmalak Hospital above a toll-free 800
number. No sound even. *Come on. Come on!*

The man said, 'I am a member of the Church of the
Resurrection and want to share my testimony with you.'

Sunless waited for the next announcements to come
from the programme, the next anything. But where were
the commercials when you needed them? Just the photograph on the screen. He felt the man's molecules stick to his

sunglasses. Why did some people have to sit so close to others? Didn't they mind?

The man's hand rummaged in his briefcase and produced another book. Sunless tried to shift an eye on to it while keeping his head straight. He saw writing in big gold letters on a navy blue cover:

The Book of Angels.

Finally, the screen reverted to regular medical programming, erasing the silence and letting him breathe freely again. The announcer's voice sounded again over a different telephone number, this time for employment at Pharmalak. The screen scrolled down the list of openings as she outlined the qualifications: medical assistant, doctor's aide, data entry specialist, medications specialist.

'Since some may not qualify for employment at Pharmalak, you should be careful of any exaggerated response to disappointment you may exhibit. Have you ever experienced jealousy when others succeed? Oversensitive to comments made about your chosen career? Envious of your partner's career progress or social contacts, even if you can't admit it? You may be suffering from Acute Envy Dysfunction, or AED. A product has been developed that may alleviate the effects of this disorder.

But Sunless was watching the book, which the man placed prominently on his briefcase, and on top of which he now arranged the two pamphlets. Sunless saw an angel depicted on the front of one. The man saw him looking and held it out to him.

'Please take it if you wish. This pamphlet outlines the origin of the Resurrection church in 1860, when Thomas Jones had his first vision.'

'He saw an angel?' Sunless was surprised at how quickly he responded and that he responded at all.

'No, not at that time. He received a vision of two figures, God the Father and Jesus Christ – here, it's in here.'

Sunless took the pamphlet and studied the picture of a young man on his knees in a grove of trees, and above him, two men floating, both about fifty, both identical: a trimmed beard and pale skin, cream robes, long hair.

'They look like the same person,' Sunless said.

'They are one god, but each have separate bodies.'

Under the picture Sunless read what one of the figures said: 'This is My Son!'

'More fathers and sons,' Sunless said.

'I'm sorry?'

Sunless took the second pamphlet, *Early Church Activity*, and studied the cover picture of a man with wings pointing to a hill.

'Is this an angel?' Sunless said.

'Yes, he is the angel who appeared to Thomas Jones in 1863, three years after Jones's first vision, and showed him where the secret gold plates were buried in the hill of Jacob.'

'An angel talked to Mr Jones?'

'And told him where he had buried the gold plates.'

'But why bury gold plates in a hill? What was up with the gold plates?'

'On those plates were inscribed true accounts of the ancient people of America, to whom Jesus Christ appeared after his resurrection. They were written by an ancient American prophet who witnessed the appearance of Jesus Christ in America. And the angel who appeared to Thomas Jones was, in fact, the son of that prophet.'

'The world tour,' Sunless said.

'What?'

'So the prophet wrote the plates, and his son became an angel, and in 1863 he showed Jones where the plates were hidden.'

'Yes, very impressive. You pick things up quickly.'

'I believe in resurrection. Where did the angel talk to Mr Jones?'

'In New York. And then he translated the plates into *The Book of Angels*,' the man said, 'which I happen to have with me, here.'

'So if I get this right,' Sunless said, 'what we've heard about Jesus is not the whole story.'

'Correct,' the man said, inching the book closer.

'And Jesus appeared in America, but it's been hushed up.'

'We believe we have the proper account of the life and appearances of Jesus,' the man said.

'That's very interesting, the real story.'

The man said, 'Did you not know that Jesus Christ appeared to the ancient peoples of America?'

'No, never heard that, though don't get me wrong. Wouldn't surprise me in the least. And all these particulars were written on the secret gold plates?'

The man smiled, arranging the pamphlets as if he had ten of them instead of two.

'They were shown to Thomas Jones.'

'I believe it.'

The man sighed. 'What you hear about our organization may not be true. We have occasionally been the subject of rumour and innuendo.'

'I know exactly what you mean,' Sunless said.

'If you like—'

'Interesting,' Sunless said. 'I'm going to read all of these very carefully. Wait, what's this — about humans living on other planets?'

'Yes, we believe that people exist on many other planets, each with its own god.'

Sunless nodded. 'I knew they had some kind of mission going on.'

'What?' the man said.

'I mean the government, not the church. I'm just putting this together in my head.'

'Well, while you think this over, may I give you this inscribed version of *The Book of Angels*?' The man lifted the large volume with both hands, as if holding a cake.

Sunless hesitated. 'Is that the same as what was written on the gold plates?'

'Exactly so, yes.'

'Okay, let me have it.' Sunless examined the book. 'Thank you. I need all the details I can get.'

The man waited a moment and said, 'Are you a believer in Jesus Christ?'

Sunless thought for a minute. The man swallowed and placed his hands on his knees, leaning forward.

'Let me ask you a question first,' Sunless said.

'Of course.'

'Do you believe in angels?' Sunless said.

The man said, 'Yes, we believe an angel appeared to

Thomas Jones. Not only that, but an angel waited at the tomb of Jesus Christ and after three days announced that he had risen.'

Sunless slouched with the pamphlets and the book. 'You're telling me an angel was at the tomb?'

'Yes, guarding the tomb.'

'Of the original Jesus?'

'There was only one.'

Sunless shook his head. 'No, I mean near the crucified body?'

'Only it was dead.'

Sunless sighed. 'That's a lot of angels suddenly, don't you think?'

The man froze. 'I don't understand.'

'I mean, the gold plates story, yes, that's believable, otherwise Jones wouldn't have found them. But why an angel at the tomb? Why would you guard a dead body?'

'I don't understand.'

Sunless pointed to the picture of the angel. 'You know, I have my own theory about angels.'

'Very well.'

'First let me tell you some more real stories, more hushed-up stories like yours. Kennedy, for instance, John F.'

The man moved an inch away from Sunless. But now Sunless wanted him to stay close, wanted to *whisper*.

'Did you know that Kennedy paid Oswald to shoot him – I mean just wound him, to give him the edge in a close election, sympathy vote, the reason Kennedy was in Dallas anyway? But Oswald slipped and fired a second shot and blew Kennedy's head off. A horrible accident.'

The man placed his hand on the book, but Sunless had it covered, moved it onto his lap.

'It's okay, I'll hold on to this,' Sunless said. 'I'm going to review it very carefully. Anyway, what Kennedy set in motion before he died was the space programme. Other planets, you see where I'm going?'

'No,' the man said.

'It all ties in with humans on other planets. Was John F. Kennedy a member of the Church of the Resurrection?'

'No, he was not.'

'Well, he certainly helped you out in 1969, because the moon landings never happened. We really went to Mars. The moon was interference. That film of the first step on to the moon is faked. It took them twenty takes in the studio because the actor in the spacesuit kept falling off the ladder. One small step, but twenty before he got his line right, and even then he got it wrong. You see where I'm going with this?'

The man shook his head and watched his book, obviously waiting for a chance to retrieve it.

'The government has everyone glued to their television sets in 1969 while a secret lander orbits Mars looking for a site, finds one, lands, and sets up a communications centre.'

'I don't think that's possible, given the technology of the time,' the man said.

'But you said Jesus appeared in America after he was dead, the angels, the gold plates. That took a bit of technology, and I believed *you*.'

'Very well, what you say is possible.' The man closed his eyes.

'A little too convenient, don't you think, that Jones gets an angel to show him the plates?'

'We would say fortunate.' The man opened them.

'Don't get me wrong, but I doubt that angels work for nothing, and your man Jones must have been some kind of genius to be able to tell that story.'

'Wait a minute—'

'No, I mean I wasn't picking on him — he was brilliant. Better than the next man at what he did.'

'It didn't sound like that just now, what you said.'

Sunless hugged the book. 'Now let me tell you another story they're keeping quiet. Ever heard of a place called Australia?'

'Yes, I have.'

'And it's clean way over on the other side of the globe. How convenient.'

'What do you mean?'

'Because Australia doesn't exist.'

'Of course it exists. I've seen pictures, it's on the map.' The man drew a circle in the air.

'Pictures? You've seen pictures? Who owns the satellite hundreds of miles up in the sky? Pictures can be manufactured.'

'Australia exists,' the man said.

'That's what you'll hear,' Sunless said. 'Two or three hundred years ago, someone comes back on a sailing ship to England and says, "I've discovered a place. It's big and far away. A lovely place, lots of space, sun shines, fruit on the trees." Once word gets out, all the strong types want to go, the adventurers, the people who could cause trouble for the government if they stayed. So the government says,

"Sure, sure, you can go." And they do, but they never come back. And people get letters saying, "Oh, it's lovely here. You should come." In future years, people get pictures of a place called Australia, news reports from Australia, Australian runners in the Olympics, strangely never winning anything. How *convenient*. But plenty of good rugby players, because, of course, the English are good rugby players. That's because the so-called Australian rugby players are English actors beamed from a studio in London. How come Australia is so like England? Can you explain that to me?'

The man smiled and stood. 'My stop is coming up. Do you think I could have the book and other material back, now that you've looked at it?'

'So you find it hard to believe that Australia is all made up?' Sunless said.

'Yes.'

'By people who said it was there and that they found it?'

'Yes.'

'But the gold plates, that's all provable, is that what you're telling me now?'

The man held out his hand. Evidently wanted his book back.

Sunless held it tighter on his lap. 'Then you have to hear my theory about angels.'

'I really don't have time,' the man said, taking his brief-case and avoiding eye contact.

'It'll only take a minute.'

'I'm sorry,' the man said, moving away toward the door. 'Some other time.'

Sunless rose and followed him step for step. 'Angels have wings and they fly around.'

The man turned. 'Look, I'm sorry about bothering you. I don't want to talk to you. This is not a good time. I'm very busy.'

'I listened to you.'

'Some other time, just not now. This is my stop.'

'You started it, and I think there's a problem with your story about angels and the dead.'

The train pulled up to the Kimball Junction station. The man stood at the door, gripping the hanging strap, his back to Sunless, who spoke as the train stopped.

'Remember the stuff about the angels with wings that fly around, always at the right place at the right time? Right beside the secret gold plates, the secret tomb of Jesus?'

'Leave me alone, will you?'

'Now what does that remind you of? *Flies*. And they call the ones closest to you guardian angels. I call them flies. A thing that flies and watches over you.'

The doors slid open. The man stepped off the train and moved away.

'Try just WATCHES YOU,' Sunless shouted.

The man did not look back.

'Angels are flies!'

Sunless shouted again as the doors slid shut.

'Angels are flies!'

SUNLESS 4

The girls who boarded the train with the church man looked first at Sunless as he went back to his seat, then at each other and giggled, hands on mouths, shoulders hunched.

Laugh away, girls. When the government fly comes for you, well, you won't be laughing, you'll be answering questions and getting into long black cars with tinted windows. You all have tracking devices in you. Sunless once pretended to be sick so that he could find out what was inside his body. The people at the hospital did a scan and told him they found nothing wrong with him. Sunless insisted on getting a copy of the film. At home, he held the scan of his body against a bulb running from a wire under his bed covers and checked for implants or spyware inside him. He found nothing.

The train turned right into the valley where, six miles away at the far end, Park City sloped along the valley floor, and above it, the Pharmalak research facility, probably busy in the mid-morning hours. Meanwhile, the girls got back to talking. Comfortable once more in his seat, Sunless turned down the volume on the video screen so he could listen in.

'I hope this trial works better than the last one,' one of them said, and Sunless looked up.

'I've been clinically depressed since I was twelve,' the girl in a blue sweater said.

'Me too,' the one with a leather jacket said and produced a pillbox. 'I'm taking these right now.'

The girl in blue read the label. 'Oh, Xanax? They're good but I gave them up after a couple of years. I'm on Zoloft. But I keep some Xanax around for when I need it.'

'I'm on Zoloft too,' the smaller of the three said. 'When I saw those commercials, I was eleven, and I pointed to the television and I told my parents, that's me. I have all those problems listed in the symptoms, like depression and social anxiety and dependency. And my doctor said I could use Prozac as well. He said I was lucky to get diagnosed so early, that some people don't get diagnosed until they are in their twenties.'

'Their twenties?' the other two said together.

'Hey, Zoloft and Prozac, I never thought of that.'

'What condition do you have?' the one in blue asked.

The smaller girl took the pillbox and said, 'I definitely have ADD, but I may have ADHD and some other developmental disorders.' She twirled a blonde braid around her finger.

'Really?' blue said. 'I must check with my doctor to see if I have those. Who's your regular doctor, apart from the drug trials?'

'It's Dr Miller, the one who's running the trial we're on.'

'That's great,' the leather girl said. 'Because I've heard he's really good with learning disorders. I had a teacher, in class one day, he looks at my learning disorders form that said I was entitled to extra time for this test he was giving, and he says, can you believe this, that I don't need it *because it's just a simple reading quiz,* and well, I called my parents straight away—'

'Didn't he get fired?'

'I think. Anyway, I must get in to see Miller as a regular patient. This first semester at college is just—'

'Me too.' The smaller girl smiled and handed the leather girl a pillbox. 'Miller's private office number is on the label. I can refer you, if you like.'

'Would you?'

'I'll give him your name.'

'Does he have a waiting list?'

Sunless turned up the volume again on his video screen. That announcer's voice – he couldn't get comfortable with it: he held his hands up to his ears to minimize any radiation or signals from the screen, across which now flashed the words 'Special Report'.

'Reports from Salt Lake City last night indicate that a gang of youths beat up some passers-by who were, according to the youths, "dressed badly and swearing". If you see any such activity, please report it to the police immediately.

'While physical violence has many causes and manifestations, you may find yourself prone to sudden bouts of extreme irritability, and in rare cases, the urge to strike out, at strangers or even a relative, for no apparent reason. Many who experience these urges have no history of aggression. If you have experienced this extreme irritability at least once per day for three weeks, you may be experiencing Sudden Irritability Syndrome, or SIS.

A related disorder is Concealed Anger Response, or CAR, a persistent but unrealized desire to cause damage.

'A product has been developed that may alleviate the effects of these disorders. On your screen is a list of participating doctors, or you can contact Pharmalak directly for further information or to obtain a pre-appointment sample.'

The screen faded with a shot of a woman throwing a glass into the fireplace and gesticulating at a man trying to hold her in an understanding manner.

The train moved across the valley. Sunless watched the green mountains rise off to his right, lined with cable-car wires and trees. No snow yet this year. Unheard of, a month into the season. The first snows should have fallen a month ago.

He stretched and rubbed the back of his neck, stiff from avoiding the church man. Above him, on the ceiling, he saw a poster, probably put there for the odd passenger who chanced to look up, whether to stretch or catch a quick nap, or maybe because he was just fed up with looking at everyone else. Whoever did happen to look up was met with a small poster showing a hand reaching for a phone:

'Have you talked to your doctor lately? Next time, ask your doctor about Elevax.'

SUNLESS 5

While staring at the ceiling, Sunless remembered that he had gone downtown recently to have his occasional tactical drink in The Ancient Mariner so that he could remain reasonably anonymous. It was one stop on the metro transit. Sunless remembered standing by the raised cantilevered tracks of the larger state-wide rail system that ran above the street. Why were those tracks so big? Plans for expansion, no doubt. Why did cities always get bigger? Plans, that's why. Plans and shovels and tracks. Sometimes people used the same words in one sentence: 'The plans are on track', or *We're tracking you, Sunless, so don't make any plans.* Sunless made a mental note to make notes on government and local authority subsidies for train tracks in the valley for the past ten years.

He remembered walking into the bar, ordering a rum and blackcurrant juice and standing exactly in the centre part of the counter where the barman pulled the draught beers, in the hope that anyone casting glances down the counter looking for someone who wished to remain invisible would ignore him standing where there was most activity.

It may have been because he had to straighten the pillow under his pullover or because the red wig tilted to one side – he had not been able to use his regular blond wig and had to spray-paint the mop, but it looked convincing, and in the strobe lights of the disco bar, who would notice anyway? Well, someone did. There's always one. A man watched him and sipped. It may have been because it was early in the evening and the strobe lights hadn't come on yet. Sunless observed him order another drink and then take a seat at the bar a few seats away. After a few tunes and another drink, the man approached him, touched his shoulder. Sunless pretended to wave at a woman on the dance floor. The dance floor, however, was empty, something he should have checked before waving.

'I saw you,' the man said.

'You saw me,' Sunless said and held his drink to shoulder height. 'And now you see me', and he drank the short and nodded to the barman.

'I saw you up there.' The man tilted a glance upward. Sunless thought he was talking about the roof of the bar, which admittedly he had climbed, but only once, to inspect it for cameras that filmed the insides of drinks and customers' breast pockets for lists and sundry items.

But the man shook his head, put down his glass and pointed through the wall.

'You were up on the mountain, up with them.'

The word 'them' lit up Sunless like an ambulance.

'Them?'

'Pharmalak, the medical crowd up in Park City. I saw you, I saw you on the train a couple of times. You went to Fargoon. You better be careful.' The man stooped to his drink.

Sunless became suspicious at the warning and shrugged,

looked around for someone to pretend to talk to. Because it was early in the evening, there was him, the other man, and the barman, who cleaned glasses with a towel over his shoulder, looking busy except that he had cleaned those glasses before. Sunless placed the drink in front of his mouth and looked the other way as he spoke from under his red wig. 'Careful?'

'The drugs. Do you know what they're really giving you? You go up there just because it's free, is that it? Are you that sick? You can't get any insurance at all?'

'You must have me mistaken for someone else.'

A couple walked in, bringing rain from the street.

The man moved a seat closer. 'You must have a twin brother then.'

Sunless watched the couple until they got uneasy and stared back.

'Yeah, anyway,' the man said, 'they've got your number. Must be a drug they're excited about. Never heard of the great Fargoon, the great psychiatrist, doing a drug trial himself.'

Another couple walked in and played the jukebox. Sunless found himself having to raise his voice, mentally that is, as he rehearsed each sentence before speaking it. He therefore decided to speak in short sentences in case the music stopped and he was caught shouting out a piece of information: 'Fargoon doesn't do them normally?'

The man shook his head. 'The word on the street is that some local doctors aren't happy. These studies are a gold mine for doctors or universities, if they can get on Pharmalak's list of approved doctors. You must have stood out to get into that study.'

'I did not,' Sunless said, 'stand out.'

'Well Pharmalak usually funds the studies, one thousand a patient, sometimes a lot more, to cover expenses. Even a small-town doctor can make a fortune. But this time the company is keeping something very close to its chest up there in the mountains.'

Sunless added up the cost of six train rides in his head. After a brief but intense period of calculation, he came to a figure lower than a thousand.

The man said, 'The company will even send a ghost-writer to help the doctor write the study findings. If the results are negative, they call in a spaceship.'

Sunless turned. 'Really?'

The man laughed with his finger pointed. 'You're listening! My name's Harry.'

Sunless eyeballed him over the rim of the glass and sipped cautiously. Too friendly. Should have given his information in a non-clandestine manner instead of sidling up to Sunless like that. Probably hired by the government to speak against the company and then to note the particulars of those who agreed with anything he said, forward them to the appropriate authorities. Sunless agreed with himself that he would have to be more careful. He left the bar but waited at the door for thirty minutes as he wrote down details of Harry's face, checking off the type of nose, forehead, mouth against a list of ten types for each facial feature so that he could reconstruct his face later, a trick he learned from an Italian drawer called Leonardo. A rain shower dripped from the letter M on the bar sign. Yes, it was raining in Salt Lake City, raining from the mountains that towered over the town. He walked back home in a straight line, his footsteps clinging to the walls as he varied the speed of his steps to avoid sending patterns into the air.

Halfway back to the metro transit station he passed an internet café and stopped in. The owner gave him a second glance and followed him to the computer terminal, pretending to ask if he wanted coffee or anything, blah blah, and went back to his desk only when Sunless gave him the sidewards look a dog does over a bone. When he was certain he wasn't being watched, Sunless pulled the wig down over his face and separated the hair at the eyes with two clothes pegs, then checked his watch.

He gave himself five minutes. Didn't want to spend too long in front of any one computer. He typed in Fargoon's name.

What came up on the monitor was lots on Fargoon in his position as Vice-President of the Organization of American Psychiatrists, also some material on Pharmalak's website, a research and development company he founded fifteen years earlier, its speciality producing psychiatric medicines for mental disorders.

Then he clicked on 'Want to Learn More about Matthew Fargoon?' He leaned to the side, out of the range of the monitor, and clicked, waited a few seconds for the flashing cameras on the other side to finish taking snapshots of the internet surfer for government records, and reviewed the list of results.

Let's see, people complaining. Of course. Alternative medicine, the league of this, the society of that. Rogue doctors charging criminal behaviour by drug companies. And so on, and so on.

The Organization of American Psychiatrists receives

advertising money and educational grants from the drug companies, amounting to millions. That made sense, Sunless thought. We help sell your stuff, we prescribe your stuff, we write about your stuff, you pay us part of what you make on that stuff. How the hell else is it supposed to work?

Another common complaint: that ADHD is a fake mental condition, and is more likely either allergies or thyroid problems or poor nutrition, and that millions of children are growing up drugged on amphetamines, and what will happen to the social and political life of the country in twenty years? In a safer environment Sunless would have written 'Nothing', but that would have meant typing on the keyboard more than was necessary and leaving even more fingerprints to clean afterwards.

Another ethical-type doctor complained that the Review Boards – supposed to evaluate psychiatric drug testing to ensure that patients weren't harmed – often had members who were paid consultants for the drug companies. Again, not a problem Sunless thought, because you need to have someone on the inside. That's only fair. Who said you leave your fate in the hands of strangers? What world do these people live in?

Another issue: family doctors were a main source for drug trials, getting paid for every patient they recruited into field research of new drugs, pushing people into studies and getting hundreds of thousands for doing it, offering a quick supply of test subjects for the drug companies. Many physicians faked the results, inventing patients and results to keep the money coming. Nothing wrong with that, Sunless noted, because you don't want to be taking advantage of sick people, do you? If healthy people take the drugs and nothing happens to them, the drug can't be all that bad. People need to think. Sunless tapped his head and luckily caught himself doing it before anyone noticed.

Having said that, Sunless hadn't taken any of the drugs Fargoon gave him after the third visit. He brought them home and once, but it was only once, he'd placed a pillbox with a month's supply of some new, experimental drug beside him on the roof, put the pills into a catapult, and one by one let them fly at people walking by on the street, bouncing them off their heads, but only at young people who hardly felt anything. Sunless wrote down the effects of each of the pills: some pedestrians appeared annoyed and puzzled, others shouted in the general direction of the sky, others scratched their heads and tried dodging movements. Some of the pills he had to tie on to small stones because otherwise they wouldn't reach the target. Okay, he had fired them from the roof more than once, a couple or three times at most, and had carefully noted the effects of the medications, conducting his own drug trials with his supply. The pills produced an effect all right. Good thing he tested them. He was glad he hadn't taken them himself.

As he was about to leave, he had an idea and typed the word 'angels' into the search box and leaned to one side to let the flashes take pictures of an empty chair. Sunless had his reasons for searching for angels, yes he had. *Let's see.* Well, well. Angels were popular. The Angel Club website, the Academy of Angels website, the Angel Message website. He selected <u>whitewhispers.com</u> and clicked on 'Introduction' under a photograph of a woman dressed in white standing beside the statue of an angel.

'Hi, I'm Angelina, and I run a service called Angel Communications, the owner and operator of <u>whitewhispers.com</u>. We facilitate contact between angels and individual souls.'

Sunless clicked on 'My Services'.

'I offer telephone consultations. First I discuss with you your particular enquiry. It may be a health concern, a question about a fiancée, or your job. Anything that concerns you enough to call me is important. I will meditate on your question under my special angel wings, made from silver threads infused with holy water, while playing angel music on my Celtic harp. In the afternoon I will call you with the message from your guardian angel. At that time I will attempt to answer any follow-up questions you may have, but please remember that most of the communications are subtle, very delicate whispers that reach me during meditation – hence the name of our company!'

Sunless clicked on 'My Office'.

'My office is entirely silver and white, the colour of the angels. White walls, white desk, silver chair, white angel telephone that chimes angel sounds when you call.'

Sunless clicked on 'My History', keeping one hand over his face in case she had a way of finding his.

'In 1983 I had a near-death experience when I fell down an escalator at a shopping mall. Rushed to the hospital, I drifted into unconsciousness and saw two angels at my bedside, standing in a shimmering light, who urged me to follow them to heaven. But I was revived. The doctors informed me that I was clinically dead for two minutes. Since my vision of the afterlife, I have learned the language of the angels. I call the delicate sounds they make "white whispering". It is these white whispers that I translate into a unique message for you straight from an angel who cares, your guardian angel. My service is one hundred per cent guaranteed. My office accepts Visa, MasterCard, and Discover.'

Sunless made notes on her claims and the types of questions she claimed most people asked of angels. 'Should I marry?', 'Should I have this operation?' All of them requests for intelligence reports, for angels to carry information between realms. The same thing they've always done, from the Old Testament to the New Testament and now to the World Wide Web. Very well, nothing had changed with the angels.

Okay, time to cover his tracks. Sunless applied for a web e-mail address, one that he could use once and throw away. Then he thought up a handle he could use once and throw away. He wrote and sent an e-mail:

> Dear Angelina, Although your site has just been
> visited by a friend, Beelzebub warns you that, even
> though you might be able to track my friend's surf
> activity to a particular location, you should attempt
> no contact with Sunless. BZB

That would scare off Angelina, a devil coming through the angel network, and scare off any angels Angelina enlisted to help locate him. Sunless was so happy with BZB for Beelzebub that he wished he could use it again. It even sounded like a fly's buzz. But that's how you get caught. Okay, Angelina in your white office, talk to the angels now. See if they want to help you now. Try finding me now.

Then Sunless reached under the table and pulled the plug, which was attached to twenty other computers, and they all went black. Twenty people shouted at the same time, some guy saying he'd lost a huge e-mail he'd been writing for the last hour. The owner boiled like a kettle and chased Sunless out on to the street. But Sunless didn't get where he was today by being easily followed. He made it to the train station and selected the seat nearest the door so that people rushing in would look above him to the empty seats they wanted. He sat in a slightly skewed fashion, pretending to sleep, and rode home in peace.

So that was the day he received his warning from Harry, i.e., the government; a formality probably, just so they could say later, when it all went bad and he was sitting in a dark room wearing sunglasses and restraints, that they had given him a fair warning. And he got his own warning off to the angels, directly into the cyberspace where they most likely lived.

SUNLESS 6

But for the shortest day of the year this was a fine morning indeed, though he noted a few clouds on the horizon. Sunless looked out the window and allowed himself to enjoy the ride as the train crawled along the valley floor on tracks set beside the main road. Not that long now to Park City. After half a mile they passed the Olympic Ski Park up the slopes on the right where dots twisted and jumped down the artificial ski runs. He had always wanted to learn to ski, to go up into the mountains around here and wind his way silently along the line of brown trees and white snow. The trouble was he would never find a time when he could do it alone: the people operating the park opened it in the morning, and that's when everyone of course arrived. Maybe he could practise skiing at night with a flashlight inserted into a band around his forehead. If the moon were out he wouldn't even need a flashlight as he skimmed over the bright snow and saw the distant mountains shine and heard nothing but the skis glide across the powder and his breath mix with the sky.

   In daylight the mountains that ringed the valley looked like brown and yellow had been burned into them by early winter, and the sky stretched its pale blue tight like a drum between the peaks. The train passed a mountain resort on the right called the Canyons, set behind a winding road: the rooftop of the main lodge rose above the trees. Underneath that roof, no doubt, people in thick red ski jackets sipped hot rum and sat in front of the lodge fireplace.

Any minute now the train would reach the open part of the valley and the final two-mile stretch to Park City before sliding into the last station, the Pharmalak building, and Sunless would in turn slide into one of the offices in that building where Fargoon sat, no doubt, reviewing his file and waiting for him, poised with his pen and his clever words, a drop of ink dangling off the tip as gravity pulled that ink into a word – or the first letter of a particular word, an S.

Well, Mr Fargoon, here comes Sunless, MD, Doctor of Survival. With a question. Hold the writing for now. No observations or diagnosis just yet, Mister Doctor Professor Fargoon.

Then Sunless saw a fly emerge from the driver's partition, circle in the air, and sail down the aisle toward him, past the girls who noticed nothing. He crouched behind the seat and reached for one of the pamphlets the man gave him, *Early Church Activity*, and rolled it because he recognized the fly as the one with the camera that read his computer screen. Sunless lowered his head. Something tickled his left hand. He lashed out with the pamphlet, but the fly rose and bounced around his head, and when he swiped again it darted off.

Then Sunless shouted, 'Try this', and rose from his seat with *The Book of Angels* above his head. Dust rode off the headrest of the seat in front as the book came down and the fly retreated a few rows to a window seat. Sunless raced up the aisle and slammed the book against the glass and then lifted it, expecting to see a stain, but the window was clean. He turned the book over. Clean as well. The fly sailed a couple of rows forward to the left aisle and hovered above the girls, who screamed as Sunless came at them shouting, 'Not going to another planet. Not today.'

The train came to a stop in Park City, and the doors slid open.

Sunless ran out. 'Not today!'

He sprinted down the platform and reached the entrance to the Pharmalak building where he ducked inside. It was a short trip to the elevator and the second floor. He checked his watch. Eleven o'clock. Right on time. And with any luck, Fargoon had seen nothing, knew nothing. And now the plan: go in, do session, find father, come out, go home.

Fargoon probably had his medicine all ready upstairs. A month's pills, a new bunch, the best on the market, brand new, great results. Yes, so good that Sunless had tried them all. When Sunless tapped lightly on the glass, Fargoon's receptionist slid back the screen and asked Sunless to sign in, looked him up and down and then motioned him to a chair in the waiting room.

'Mr Fargoon will be with you shortly.'

He sat on a white chair and wiped his forehead with his sleeve. His skin swam hot and wet and his shirt fastened to his back with sweat; the skirmish with the fly left him breathing hard. He tried to breathe deeper, but before he had time to compose himself she came out holding a folder.

'Mr Fargoon will see you now.'

Sunless smelled wood polish as he walked the burgundy rug to his suite, and when the receptionist opened the door for him and stood aside, he saw Fargoon sitting behind his oak desk reading a file. The light was still low and soft and the books on the shelves gleamed yellow under the desk lamp. The green plant had grown further up to the windowsill. Mr Fargoon wore his usual white linen suit and blue tie, and he stood and came around the desk as Sunless walked to the chair.

'Good morning. I missed you last month.' The hand was out and Fargoon's head was tilted to one side, perhaps because of his wide smile, perhaps because of the big question in his head, which he asked after withdrawing his damp hand:

'You look very tired, exhausted I'd say. Are you sweating?'

'I am.' Sunless sat, wiping his forehead. The fish in the painting, he noted, was still without a sea, and the plant still reached for the light of the window. Fargoon motioned him to sit down.

'What type of fish is that?' Sunless said.

Fargoon opened the folder. 'I have no idea I'm afraid.' Fargoon raised his eyebrows and slowly walked around to his side of the desk. His shoes made no sound on the carpet and he straightened his jacket in silence as the clock ticked and Sunless sweated more.

'I can well understand,' Fargoon said, taking a tissue from a box near his calendar, 'if there's a problem.' He dried his hand.

'See if you can guess what's wrong with me.'

'I don't know, but I can see you're sweating as if you've been running. Perhaps from something?'

Sunless closed his eyes. 'I was followed here.'

'And you were followed by?'

'By a fly.'

Sunless opened his eyes as Fargoon sighed. 'Oh, not that fly again—'

'He's out there.'

'But haven't we heard enough of that fly by now, flies in general?' Fargoon reached across the desk with a tissue. Sunless dabbed his face as Fargoon opened his file.

'You don't know.' Sunless dropped the tissue into the waste basket.

'What I know,' Fargoon said glancing at a page, 'is that you've been coming here for six months, we've been having conversations, and I just don't know what this fascination is with flies. It's all very interesting from a professional point of view, but I wonder—'

Sunless coughed and felt the sweat turn cold. 'You mean the significance.'

'Yes.' Fargoon turned a page.

'They're following me. That's the significance. At the end of the world the angels come with the bowls of plagues and everything and blow the seven trumpets and the dead rise up, all that's left of them anyway. It's all about death. Angels run everything. That's the revelation. They don't serve anyone, and they don't live downstairs. They stole Jesus and they steal other things too; they take what they want. They divided up heaven and earth between them on the second day – couldn't wait to get going, the lot of them. They're prowling.'

'Many people are quite fond of angels,' Fargoon said. 'That's an interesting view, prowling.'

'I'm not found by angels.'

'What did you say?'

'I said I'm not fond of angels.'

Fargoon wrote more and put the file down and stood. 'So is the fly here now? A December fly? Waiting outside? Should I check the hallway?' He raised his left arm.

'Of course not, that's absurd. The fly wouldn't follow me up here. It would never get out again.'

Fargoon sat again and sighed again. 'Very well.'

'And I think it has something to do with someone who's gone missing.'

Fargoon raised an eyebrow.

Sunless said, 'But that's another matter. I have a question for you.'

'Of course, and then we have to get moving with today's session.' Fargoon smiled as he tapped his wristwatch. Then he coughed precisely, like slicing an onion.

Sunless placed both hands on his lap. 'My father is missing, and I think you know where he is. Do you know where he is?'

Fargoon appeared to freeze in place, his left hand in the act of turning another page in the file, a fresh page no doubt, for writing on. Then he laid the file flat and twisted the top off his fountain pen.

Sunless wasn't going to fill in the silence this time. He turned to the window. Fargoon's office had a good view of the mountain slopes, and Sunless watched a copse of trees about two hundred yards away, midway up the nearest mountain trail. A couple of hikers walked past it on their way to the summit. He refocused when a stain landed on the window, and he saw that the stain was a snowflake, and then he looked up at the sky and realized it had clouded up. A shadow passed across Fargoon's office and the desk lamp shone brighter. Sunless felt the cold on him, felt the sweat chill to a second skin.

The doctor spoke. 'You've never asked me that question before.'

Sunless turned to him. 'I did.'

'No,' Fargoon shook his head, 'no – I'd remember. I have these notes.' He held up the folder, an inch thick with papers. 'This is everything you've said to me for six months.'

'I see what you're showing me.'

'All photocopied, and you have never,' Fargoon stood, 'you have never asked me that question.'

'I wanted to then.'

'Have you been taking your medication, Sunless?'

'I have the pills. I have them.' Sunless patted his pocket.

'Have you swallowed them?'

'Yes.'

'You're sure?'

'I'm sure I just said yes.'

Sunless had taken a few early on but then used them with the catapult on the pedestrians and wrote the effects of the pills on an index card before every visit to Fargoon, making sure his symptoms were slightly better or worse each time to be convincing.

Fargoon moved his chair forward. 'Let's begin. Your condition, please.'

And Sunless spoke for twenty minutes or thereabouts about the effects of the previous medicine.

When he finished, Fargoon tore off a piece of paper. 'Now this is what's wrong with you.'

Sunless read one word: CGAS.

'I have sea–gas?'

'No, anxiety.'

'Anxiety? That's all that's wrong with me after all this time?'

'Chronic Generalized Anxiety Syndrome. Never been clearer,' Fargoon said. 'I need to put you on a new medication to calm you down a little, to give you a chance to rest and come to terms with what's happened.' Then he wrote out a prescription. 'Here, take this down to the pharmacy.'

Sunless read one word, Elevax, under Fargoon's name.

'This cures worry about what doesn't exist?'

'Life can be difficult, Sunless,' Fargoon said, rising. 'You are here for that reason.'

Sunless rose too, folded the prescription, and put it into his pants pocket. 'I have another question,' he said.

'Yes?' Fargoon moved his blue tie.

'I was wondering where anxiety comes from. It's everywhere I look, billboards, television, and it's spreading.'

Fargoon stared at Sunless a moment and turned to the shelves of book and rubbed some with his hand. 'We're looking for anxiety, too,' he said. 'We would be very interested in locating it. Very interested indeed.'

'So you don't know where it is.'

'I didn't say that.' Fargoon maintained his smile. 'It's complicated science. Many companies, a worldwide effort, but I think we're doing quite well.'

'My second question—'

'Yes—'

'I already asked. My father. Where is he?' Sunless placed his hands by his side and faced Fargoon, who in turn walked to Sunless's file and closed it in one movement. 'You have never asked that question before, and today I hear it twice. Is there a reason?'

Sunless shrugged. 'I forgot to ask before. Kept leaving your office without bringing it up, and halfway down the hall I'd kick myself because I forgot. He's somewhere in this building.'

'Did you read the letter?' Fargoon said.

'I read no letter. What letter?'

'I believe we sent a letter on Saturday afternoon.'

'I got no letter.'

Fargoon seemed to think a moment before removing the bulge from his jacket pocket and twirling a pillbox in his hands.

'For a few months – after you first came here – I pre-scribed you sedatives, because you needed them after what happened.' He placed the pills on the corner of his desk. 'After three months, and until now, these are what you've been taking. I couldn't give you anything for what you suffered from. You were taking sugar pills; that is, placebos under various names.'

Sunless sat again. 'So all those names of diseases, you made them up?'

Fargoon smiled his teeth loudly and shook his head quickly.

'All very real conditions, all too real, and we are con-ducting drug trials involving many patients. I broke the double blind and put you on a placebo.'

'If there was nothing in the pills, what—?'

'I thought I might let you talk, just talk, sometimes that's the pill, you see.'

Sunless leaned forward and scanned Fargoon's desk. 'It's just as well, I didn't take them anyway.'

When the doctor said nothing, Sunless continued, 'Why aren't you writing any of this down?'

'Not today.'

'I'd like you to do that, even if it's for the last time, Mr Fargoon.'

'Very well.' Fargoon sat behind the desk and opened his pad, held the pen and set it in the air above the line at the top of the page. 'Yes?' he said without looking up.

'How long do we have?' Sunless said.

'At most fifteen minutes. I have a lecture to give at three and then a few hours up here, finishing work before the holidays. You know, one's work is never done.' He waved at the ceiling and sighed, sifted some pages from the folder and handed them to Sunless. 'Here are the photocopies of the notes from our last session. Take them and put them with the others.'

'Okay.'

'You have other notes from our sessions, am I right?'

'I have them all, I've seen them all around the house. Okay, I'm ready.'

Sunless leaned back in his chair and looked out the window.

In the day's last light Sunless noticed how the clouds had gathered like black cotton over the mountains. On the slopes, a string of lights led the way up to one of the ski lodges; people were carrying skis. Snow was in the air. In the morning, the ski lifts would bring people to the mountain top for the first full day of the season. Reports of Christmas in the air, children soon running to their parents with what they found under the tree. Sunless felt the emptiness of the holiday leak into him and spread like ink into his eyesight and stain the world. From now until spring and the thaw, Park City would fill each and every evening with meals and cocktails and fireplaces. He looked at Fargoon in his white suit, wondered about the man's own children and whether he had any.

And as Sunless began to speak, Fargoon began to write. Never looked up, did Fargoon, except that once, when Sunless talked about the October flies and a couple of other times. He didn't look up because he had to keep up with Sunless.

'I am Sunless. I am a dead man. I have a father and a mother. I never met them. I have a brother I do not know, but he showed me pages once that taught me how to breathe when I was alive and I did see them through my mother's skin but I was born without breathing and that is why I can talk for ever with one breath and I am making this up and the whole world up and nothing is real till I find who made me even if I was not made well enough to live and this is still the same breath, the one I never had.

'What I'd like to know is why I never had a future, why it never came for me. At least I could have said no, no thanks, I don't want a future. I'd like to know who stole it, even if it doesn't exist. Instead I got the glass room in heaven, I got to see how the happy ones live but couldn't reach them. Look: they can't see me. And you can't see me, can you?'

Fargoon wrote without commenting.

'See?' Sunless said.

He watched the mountain whiten and the snow on the sill grow to half an inch. And Fargoon, he sat and waited, occasionally sipping from a glass of water. Sunless heard a clock. Sunless heard snow.

It was falling again, flakes captured in the house and cabin lights across the mountainside and into the woods and fields. Angels were prowling, their wings spreading shadows across the face of the sky, shadows that held more snow. They knew where he was now. Minutes till the end, at most. They'd smash through the window and take him. They didn't waste time because they had none to waste. They were brutal and fast and they were all business. They'd spy him in Fargoon's office through the window.

Sunless saw the seconds fade like a condemned man. 'I want my dad back. Give him back. Give him back now.'

'Almost ready,' Fargoon said. He put his pen on the desk and tore off the two pages he'd written and went to the photocopier. After the copies slid on to the tray, he handed the originals to Sunless.

'Take these with you and put them with the others,' he said.

Sunless folded the notes and put them into his pocket.

'And Jane, who will meet you downstairs in the café in about thirty minutes, will bring you to your father,' Fargoon said. 'She'll take care of you from here. By the way,' he waved his pen, 'will you be needing another prescription?'

'No.' Sunless moved away from the window, out of easy

reach. He watched Fargoon close his folder and felt gratitude for the hours alone in this office. Fargoon spoke into his intercom and asked for coffee.

'You know, I like you Sunless. And what your father did for us – it's because of men like him that science progresses as it does. But I did remove you from the trials because I guessed you weren't taking your medications, and in a way I didn't want you to.'

'Some of those things made me feel strange, the ones I tried at the beginning.'

'They were new, very new.' He stood, 'Follow me, will you?' and he pointed Sunless down a different hallway to his receptionist's office. 'In here, please.' As Sunless walked with him, Fargoon touched Sunless on the shoulder, 'Do you know that I haven't had coffee today at all? My wife keeps telling me to give it up.'

'Will you give it up then?' Sunless said.

'I keep telling her I will. But I could do with a cup, especially when I feel a lecture coming on. I have to give one at three.'

He motioned Sunless along. This hall was smaller, the walls an ice green, and posters were tacked every few feet. One showed a young girl standing under a cloud: 'Think you're depressed?' A few feet farther, the same girl stood under bright sunshine with a cell phone in one hand and a passport in the other: 'Or do you feel energized?' Sunless guessed there was a number three. A few steps more, and there it was, third in line. This one showed the girl split down the middle, half in shadow, half in sunlight, her mouth half drooping and half smiling. Behind her some children played on a playground seesaw. The caption above read: 'Maybe you have bipolar disease. Ask your doctor about Elevax, a new product for bipolar disease from Pharmalak.'

Fargoon said, 'That's our new marketing campaign. I like to be involved in all aspects of drug research, development and promotion. In a sense, they're all part of the production line. Some drugs sell themselves, some you have to sell. And conditions change. Depression as a disease has outlived its usefulness.' He smiled at Sunless. 'You, for instance, you're more the bipolar type, more a touch of the up and down with you, my friend – I've seen you often very withdrawn and then sometimes, like today, very enthusiastic; a few years ago, even two, you might have been labelled incorrectly. Now we have four classes of bipolar.'

'I thought I used to be schizophrenic.'

The receptionist walked toward them along the ice-green paint of the walls and handed Fargoon his coffee.

'No – not at all,' the good doctor said. 'I was evaluating possibilities. Bipolar is a sequence: hypomania, where you pun too much, talk too much, do everything too much, and its opposite – complete withdrawal, utter withdrawal from the world.' Fargoon tapped the third poster with an approving finger.

'Elevax,' he said. 'Keep your eye on that one – a mix of anticonvulsants and lithium, and as we discover more classes of bipolar, we'll adapt the drug. I'm certain we'll be seeing ten classes within two years. Our vision,' he said.

'Vision?' Sunless said.

'A drug for every mood.'

Sunless removed his sunglasses, but the narrow green

hall crowded in on him and he put them back on, saying as Fargoon drank from his cup:

'I have a definition of Paranoid Schizophrenia for you.'

'But you don't have that condition, I told you.'

'Paranoid Schizophrenia is when you make two of your-self in case they get one of you.'

Fargoon held the cup in midair as if balancing it for the right words. 'You know, sometimes I don't know whether to laugh or cry when I listen to you.' He appeared to be lost for more words and drank from his coffee again, straight-ened his blue tie, studying the poster of the girl split in two on the wall.

The doctor scratched his head. 'Who is this *Sunless*, may I ask?'

'I am not Sunless.'

'Ah, a disguise,' the doctor smiled. He walked to the receptionist's door and called for her while nodding at Sunless. She appeared with a pencil and notebook.

'Please show Sunless how to get to the café.' Then Fargoon walked over to Sunless and held out his hand.

'You can go there now and wait, if you wish. We'll have everything ready for you. I think that you will feel better today. I know that we will have your father for you today.'

Fargoon held out his left arm in his white suit and Sunless walked to the outside waiting room where the receptionist then reached out her own arm to guide him to the door that led to the main hall, where he sometimes waited if the waiting room was occupied. But before he followed her arm, Sunless held open the office door that she wanted to close.

'Doctor, you don't believe in angels, do you?'

Fargoon was already standing back in his own office by the window observing the gathering clouds. He did not turn around as Sunless continued, 'Or that angels are flies. But they do exist, and they're out there.'

'Thank you,' Fargoon said.

At the end of the hall, the receptionist handed him a map she had drawn of how to get to the café.

'It's to the right of the entrance lobby,' she said.

Sunless checked his watch as he passed the pharmacy without stopping. Twelve noon. To hell with the pharmacy. Maybe Fargoon called ahead for Sunless to get Elevax the special edition: one pill and you're on your way, worries over. Keeping close to the wall, Sunless walked the stairs down to the lobby. No point in getting cornered in the elevator by two orderlies forcing mouthfuls of Elevax into him.

Downstairs he found the café on the other side of the lobby but decided to go outside, since Fargoon expected him to wait in the café. The first words you should hear at birth: welcome to the world, and always do the opposite of what people expect. As he reached the pavement he saw more people wearing overcoats and felt how much the morning had chilled. That could happen in the mountains. He felt his light jacket around him and made for the slopes; no way was he hanging around Pharmalak for four hours. Today was the day he would find out where the missing went, where his father was, where the secret laboratory was, and what Fargoon had in his files.

The fresh air woke him up as Sunless headed up the slope to the copse of trees he'd seen from Fargoon's widow, and when he reached them he lifted out the mini-binoculars he carried in his coat pocket and swept the area. *Don't put my file away just yet, Fargoon.* Yes, keep one eye to the window, because you know I'm not going to wait in your trap: this is Sunless. You should know what I can do. I've told you other things.

Now relatively safe at three hundred yards from the facility, he scanned the valley while delivering a report to himself.

December 21. MONDAY, twenty minutes past noon. Finished appointment with Fargoon in Park City. Now keeping low in woods until next meeting. Fargoon aware. Reviewing options.

To his left on the lower slope by the approach road to Park City, about ten people picked their way along a trail. Sunless watched as they wound across the side of the mountain like a zip, swinging their arms and chatting. The runners reached the tree line near Pharmalak, led by a man in black running pants and a pink sweater, very quick on his feet, looking about him as he ran. His face looked like it was pulled down by weights, his eyes too, like a monk's, from a history book. The pink man led the group through the trees and into the mountain resort of the Pharmalak hospital. Sunless could not follow him because of the trees, so he moved his binoculars right, to Park City at the bottom of the slope. The main street was a half mile long, old stores and houses, restaurants, a cinema, a bookstore, surrounded on three sides by smaller hills with houses.

West of the town lay open ground, and there he saw the

condos in horseshoe-shaped developments, one behind the other, rows and rows of bungalows with orange roofs and lawns cut to a tight green. He brought the binoculars back to the olive and brown building of Pharmalak. And on the second floor, the third room from the right, the glint of the sun in one window and what he thought was Fargoon's figure, looking out at the valley.

The snowflakes on the doctor's window had friends. They were falling now, lacing the grass on the mountain-side with white. Just as fast, however, a gust blew and sunlight chased them away. There was a war going on in the sky. Sunless stood at the woods' edge and looked west. Dark, heavy cloud ringed with afternoon sun brushed across the blue, and rays of brilliant sunlight spread out from behind them, like spokes on wheels. The breeze moved across the mountainside and into the woods, and the leaves tinkled like glass around him. Sunless raised his binoculars and scanned the clouds for signs of activity. This was the type of weather where you'd have things patrolling the skies, looking down.

He'd read in the Old Testament, where all the angry angels were, how a witness observed in the distance a bright cloud coming from the north, a heavy cloud, bright in the centre and ringed with light at the edges. A chariot approached with four angels facing outward, and each angel had four faces, and although the angels moved, their knees remained straight and stiff, and each angel had four arms, two on each shoulder, one set stretched above, the other covering the body. And over their heads, balanced on their wings, a giant crystal ball.

Sunless, you've been reading too many Bibles, he said to himself.

Too many rays of sunshine coming out of the clouds, too many wings coming down, orders being passed on. Orders and more orders: orders in the heavens, orders on earth, orders of people, orders of angels, orders to do, orders not to do; orders to come, orders to leave, orders to eat, orders to fast. We must have order. We must have orders. We must have ordering.

But that angel chariot now haunted him as it trawled the sky and the mountainside with its big eye: *We see you, Sunless.* We can see in all directions. We'll come for you again any day now. Hide all you want to. We're up here watching you and we'll catch you out in the open, and that will be the end of Sunless again. And the wheels spun the rays of light through the clouds as the chariot moved to the centre of the sky, closer and closer. Sunless followed with his lens. There, that cloud, that cloud was moving toward him, the wheels roiling the heavenly vapours behind them.

Sunless instantly blended back into the trees – and in a moment his face was lost in the lines of bark from where he searched the sky for the chariot. The cloud had reached the point in the sky directly over the trees. Sunless froze, hoping for camouflage. He should have read the Bibles a lot more carefully and then he would have been ready for this. Like the part where another revelation happened, and from another cloud too, of course:

> And I saw another mighty cloud come down from
> heaven, pierced on the right and on the left side
> with silver wings. And under the cloud I saw legs
> glow as if on fire, and then the wings fluttered and
> the cloud parted, and I saw a rainbow in the shifting

vapours. Yes, I saw that its head was a mighty circling eye flashing in the sun. And then two legs pierced the cloud, and two more, until the cloud was gone, and a winged creature hovered. It held a little scroll in one of its legs. I approached and pulled the scroll from the *puvilli*, the pincers at the feet, and unrolled it, and read: 'Thou shalt have no strange flies before me.'

Sunless stepped back and lowered his binoculars. He wasn't being chased by flies. He was being chased by angels, and if they were half as good as flies, angels would be damn good at finding people. Flies can smell murder a mile away, and although he, Sunless, personally knew nothing about murder, he knew that flies get there before anyone else, before the person is cold; and when the police arrive, the first thing they'll sometimes do is gather and test the flies for clues. If they could, flies might offer testimony. 'We flew in twenty minutes after death, approximately three days before human discovery. We proceeded to chart the body. She was dead three days before humans found her.' The smart detective has flies on a leash sailing ahead of him in the air. Cry havoc! Let slip the flies of crime! Let's find Sunless. Sunless where are you? What did you do? Oh, that's all right, we'll find out ourselves! Yeahh!

Sunless looked fearfully at the sky, the wide and open sky.

He could defend himself, construct crossbows, cannon, catapults, send fire back at them and their long swords, those Old Testament angels that don't come to talk but to kill. He'd make fifteen miniature Sunlesses, exact copies, and run out into the open, scattering himself to the four winds and firing in all directions. Yes, find the real Sunless now. Bang bang.

But all that fell from the sky toward him was bits of snow, covering the world and Sunless, the world of Sunless. He searched the right side of the sky, still fine and sunny, though the cloud was drawing a curtain across the valley from the other side, pulled by the chariot and the determined angels with swords who had followed him all the way from the lake. They had been watching all the time. They knew what he'd done. That big eye in the sky had seen everything, and now he would be taken up.

Then he shook his fist and shouted, 'You will not find me again. I'm getting rid of the future anyway, so you'll have nowhere to catch me.'

He walked deeper into the woods until he came to a clearing lightly dusted with snow on the webs of tree branches. Good – he was invisible here. He put his head to one side like a duck looking for hawks. (Dangerous things, clouds, no telling what could come out of them.) Taking up a fallen branch, he trained it at the sky where he last saw the chariot cloud, to breach the vapours and see the angels. But the chariot was nowhere to be seen.

As Sunless searched with his telescope more snow fell until it cloaked him in white. All the more difficult now to spot him. Three hours to the showdown with Pharmalak.

MONDAY, 1.03 p.m. Snow falling. Activity in sky above woods. Some lights coming on in Pharmalak building and in Park City. Temperature down in last twenty minutes.

Brushing the snow off a bough, he sat down. Park City had grown yellow with all the Christmas lights on Main Street, and people crossed the streets with shopping bags. He panned the valley with his binoculars. The snow had stopped again, but now there was a coating on the ground that the wind couldn't blow off. He saw people carrying skis gathered at the bottom of the slope and spoke to himself again as he searched up the building to Fargoon's office, where the blinds had been drawn, then moved back into the clearing and sat again on his bough.

What to do? His mind raced with visions. What would he do till four o'clock? He looked at himself and saw that he wore a coat of white. Small wonder, since he had been trained by the best man in the business, Mr Fargoon, and had spent much personal time with him. His own office was ready now; he had a table and chairs, and all he needed was a speciality. No problem, he could specialize in anxiety: Sunless, Doctor of Anxiety, or better still Dr Sunless, anxiety specialist. Welcome to a day in the office of Dr Sunless. He imagined erecting a sign on the path: 'You get the ills, you bring the bills, I have the pills.'

A patient walks along the path, a 40-year-old woman, married with two children, excellent career, walks confidently but with yes, a hint of anxiety. Sunless watches her and notes, *She's read something, has an air of a little information*, and says, 'Good afternoon. How can I help you today?'

She says, 'Yes, I think I may have CGAS.'

'Come again?'

'CGAS, Chronic Generalized Anxiety Syndrome.'

Sunless sits back. 'And what makes you think that?'

She hasn't even sat down herself, never mind said hello,

and now she sighs. She doesn't like his response. Sunless should be already writing the prescription on his pad, not asking her questions like that.

She already has the name of the drug on a piece of paper. 'I read up on the symptoms, and I'm concerned. I'd like to take something for it.'

'Did you see a commercial on television that said, "Talk to your doctor"?'

'I read up on it, on the internet, as a matter of fact.'

'And?'

'And I'm concerned.'

Sunless looks away and runs his glasses up his nose with his fingertip. Of course, she thinks she's the first one.

'Please describe your symptoms.'

'I avoid social situations, I can't relax when people come visiting, and I'm anxious all the time.'

'What's wrong with that?'

'What?'

'Avoiding people, that's a healthy sign, isn't it?'

'No – that's bad. I don't understand.'

'So the *television* said you have CGAS, right?'

'No, I said I read up on it on a medical reference site, a popular one.'

'Drugsatyourfingertips.com, right?'

'Actually, no, and will you please stop saying *right*? And I want to treat this disorder. I want to try Elevax because I'm concerned.'

'No—'

'Excuse me, what did you say?'

'No, I don't want to prescribe you Elevax, and I don't want to talk about Chronic Generalized Anxiety Syndrome, which I know the television told you to say to me.'

'But I—'

'You could have ASS, Aggravated Sensitivity Syndrome. Sounds like that to me.'

'No, I don't have ASS. I have CGAS.'

'Were you followed here?' Sunless gets up and checks behind her, observes the path in the woods for movement.

'What?' she says.

'Were you followed?'

'I don't know.' She looks concerned now.

'So you're not anxious about that possibility.'

'No. I'm anxious about this conversation.'

'Even though I just asked you about being followed.'

'I said I didn't know if I'm being followed.'

'But you look concerned.'

'I'm not!'

Sunless shakes his head and takes off his glasses, looking serious now. 'So you don't *know* if you were followed here, but you aren't concerned; yet you *think* you might have Chronic Generalized Anxiety Syndrome, and that really concerns you. Is that what you're telling me?'

'You are offending me,' she says.

Sunless nods. 'That may be true. But you're the one who came to me. People could be watching you and that doesn't bother you at all, so there's absolutely nothing wrong with you. Go home and come back when there's something wrong with you.'

She's gone. And from the moment she came into the office, she never once looked behind her. Not a care in the world. Nothing wrong with the woman.

★

Sunless looked around and felt the cold come through the trees. He shivered. Didn't plan for an evening lying in the woods in December in the mountains. He should have worn warmer clothes today when he knew he was coming up into the mountains. As the sun dropped lower, the woods grew shadows around him. Walking back to the edge of the woods, he saw that the lights had spread across the windows of the facility, and in Fargoon's office also, behind the drawn blinds. What are you doing right now, Fargoon? Finishing up for the day?

The lights were all bright in Park City too: he watched people on Main Street move from store to store, but then he heard a sound and looked up to see above the trees, there, swooping above the trees with the grinding noise of wheels turning, riding right above the woods, Ezekiel's chariot.

Sunless dove on to the ground and cast a terrified eye skyward. The chariot moved slowly overhead, ploughing the skies, looking for him. He hoped that the snow concealed him where he lay. The chariot passed. He was about to get up again when another chariot flew in. Sunless closed his eyes to ready himself for the beginning of the End Times. But the noise passed, and then he chanced a glance and saw the wires, a cable car bringing skiers up the mountain.

He sat up and let his heart calm before standing. Sunless thought about living in a world lit just by the moon and the stars and the snow. The moon by day, the stars by night. No sun. No room for the sun.

MONDAY, 2.14 p.m. Activity in town. Most

lights have come on in the facility. Fargoon's office active. Blinds drawn. Skiing has commenced on slopes.

He swept the area with his binoculars. More activity on Main Street in Park City. The Christmas tree at one end of the street glowed yellows and reds, and the shuttle buses picked up skiers who had begun to come out of their hotels. Sunless checked the sky again. In the streets, people clapped their hands together and smiled. One or two pointed up. And the snow fell heavier, large flakes, as the mountain turned completely white, and so did Park City, and so did the whole world, and in it, Sunless. And he was turning white, disappearing into that world.

At that point he remarked to himself that Pharmalak looked slightly bigger, swollen. And the disturbances in the air seemed concentrated more now around and above the building itself. Little orange streaks in the sky, flashes, pieces of ash. And then a man from the bushes at the side of the building waved at him. There he was, over there. Who the hell was waving at him? Who could see him here? Sunless trained his binoculars on the bushes. It was Harry, the man from the bar. He was pumping a machine that belched smoke and had flames licking out the sides of it, a machine connected with pipes to a window and a steel door. And he was waving up the mountainside at Sunless. Was he telling him to come down or just saying hello? Sunless tried to read his lips, he was saying some-thing like 'I know what you did', or was it 'I'm going to blow up the world'?

But that reminded Sunless of something. He sat back

and unfolded a letter from his pocket. Yes, of course, something on his list for today: 'Your father's remains will be cremated on the afternoon of December 21. Burial will be at 7.00 p.m. that evening in Salt Lake City Municipal Cemetery. Please contact us for details and to make any special arrangements.' So that's what Harry was doing. Sunless knew there'd be more of these atmospheric problems. He needed to conceal himself fully and so breathlessly removed his jacket and shirt, put back on his jacket, and scraped snow off the leaves and dug some dirt out of the ground and placed them in the middle of the shirt, which he then wrapped around his head, making sure it also fit snugly around his ears. Anyone searching from above would not see a white shirt over white ground, and the dirt would stop any radioactive signatures leaking from his brain into the air. The art of being invisible. Not an easy thing to perfect, he once told Fargoon. When Sunless asked him if he'd ever been invisible, Fargoon said nothing, naturally, and kept writing. 'It takes practice,' Sunless told him. You can live beside and around people for days and weeks and months and years and they won't see you, not if you don't want them to. If you're well camouflaged you could move among them and they won't see you. 'No,' Sunless told Fargoon, 'I don't get out much, bit of a recluse, but you get used to it. The television is a blessing, the windows are your eyes, the doors your ears, the house tells you everything, channels all the information from outside. You don't have to do anything at all.'

He pulled the shirt tighter; there, now I'm the shirt-and-dirt man. He walked out of the woods and down the slope.

Why wait until four o'clock? That's what Fargoon
expected – I'll go to the café right now. He crunched in the
snow because the entire valley was coated in silence; in
that case he'd have to walk carefully and then nobody
would hear his steps. To his right, three skiers turned their
skis at the end of their run and came to a halt. Sunless
looked over and waved. One of them waved back, and
they all shuffled his way, their breath ballooning steam. The
first lifted his ski goggles.

'Are you okay?' he said.

Sunless stopped. 'Guess what's wrong with me, if I'm not
okay.'

He said, 'You're wearing a shirt on your head and you've
got leaves and dirt sticking out the sides, and that's just for
starters, man.' A second man laughed. They moved with
Sunless down the slope.

'Let's go,' a woman said. She kept her goggles on and followed behind.

'Are you hurt?' the first man said. 'Something with your
head?'

'I'm on my way to the café,' Sunless said. 'And I would-
n't be seen talking to me if I were you.'

'Why not?'

Sunless pointed up. 'You'll betray my position. A bunch
of them out flying today. There's a reason why *eye* and *sky*
rhyme.'

The men looked into the sky and then at each other.

Sunless added, 'Yes, it does look like more snow.'

'Yes,' the second one said.

'Yes,' Sunless said, moving faster, 'I think we're in for
some weather. And I can tell my future.'

'You can, so what is it?' the second man said as the woman poked him in the back.

'I don't have one.' And Sunless shuffled down to the Pharmalak building, occasionally ducking and weaving, never looking up.

Sunless 7

As he reached the Pharmalak complex, Sunless felt the heat
and witnessed more disturbances in the sky. The building
looked bigger, and around it tiny orange streaks flitted in
and out of a deepening mist, so small they were gone as
soon as he noticed them. Sunless trailed his fingers along
the walls of the building. Yes, they were hotter, but Harry
and his pump were gone. Sunless wondered if the same
strange events were occurring in Salt Lake City. Running
away from the skiers had made the shirt with the dirt on his
head loosen and tip to one side, so before entering the
facility, Sunless adjusted himself and then went in with the
air of someone busy, while making a show of looking at his
watch. Looking busy was a great way to stay unnoticed.
Once inside the reception area he climbed the stairs to the
top of the building. There was that orange glow out to the
west again, even though he could not see the city itself. Was
this the End Times? Was the city on fire, the streaks of light
really angels pouring the bowls of plague? If so, people
would be disappearing everywhere about now. He ran
down the stairs and noticed how hot the steps were under
his feet. As he tiptoed along a corridor he felt warm air
blow from a room and entered.

★

When Fargoon's giant head greeted him on a projector screen, Sunless involuntarily ducked.

'Good afternoon. My name is Matthew Fargoon, and I am president of the company.'

'Close the door, please,' someone whispered.

Sunless closed it as Fargoon's head, three feet tall on the screen, spoke to a dark room of heads shaved in the projector light. And what big eyes Fargoon had, too.

Sunless found himself in a long dark lecture hall with forty or fifty people and a stage up front on which a dais and microphone stood, and behind it, yes, the one and only Mr Fargoon. In the back, a large screen projected his image. So there were two Fargoons, a small and big version. The man would need to take something for that.

Fargoon coughed, wiped his hand with a tissue, and shuffled some papers. Sunless crept to the back of the hall. A man with a white coat and clipboard looked him up and down. Sunless straightened the shirt on his head and folded his arms and leaned against the back wall as if he were stopping by for a few minutes. 'Sir,' the man said. When Sunless turned, the man pointed to his own head. Sunless wondered what was wrong with him. Then he unwrapped the shirt from his head and shook the dirt loose on to the floor. The man in the white coat seemed to mimic this by shaking his head also. Sunless deliberated whether it was a sign of disapproval and concluded that the man was simply exercising his neck muscles, which a lot of people did when he was around.

Fargoon said, 'Welcome, everyone, to the final meeting of Pharmalak's winter company representative training programme. That's quite a lot to say already, isn't it?'

Someone laughed.

'I hope you all had pleasant flights into the Salt Lake region this morning. In the first three sessions today you learned why Pharmalak is a unique institution, combining a private research and development corporation with modest hospital facilities for those who can afford our services and a vigorous and successful patient outreach programme that allows us to conduct drug trials. You are here today because we intend to expand our drug testing programmes nationally. Yes, I can announce that Pharmalak is going truly nationwide and—'

The room broke into applause. Sunless clapped too, and smiled too, since the claps sounded like people were smiling.

'Nationwide,' people said, clapping and cheering.

'Nationwide,' Sunless said, clapping and nodding.

Fargoon held up a hand — 'and that we have indeed developed what we think is our breakthrough therapeutic drug, Elevax.'

'Elevax,' some people said and clapped and were instantly joined by the rest of the room. Again Sunless clapped and cheered.

'Let's begin this session by handing you over to Max, our testing coordinator. Max, take the stand please.'

Fargoon stepped to one side as a thin man pulled the microphone lower and said, 'I'll keep this short, as it's been a long day. Please go to your group leaders and form into the same discussion groups as you had this morning. Your group leaders will distribute the questionnaires we discussed.'

Sunless was about to leave when the lights stung his

eyes like a slap. He automatically shielded his face. People moved chairs. Someone said, 'Excuse me' and brushed his leg.

Max continued, 'As company reps you are the human face of Pharmalak's products, and especially now of our new drug. I remind you that the questionnaire you have been given is a self-discovery device, a mirror of your skills as a company representative. Direct selling may not be far off as politicians overcome restrictive trade practices and open up health commerce. There's the Avon Lady, the Tupperware party, now get ready for the Ritalin coffee group, the Elevax book club.'

Some people laughed. Sunless dropped his hand from his face and saw a group of three forming right beside him, two men and a woman.

'To prepare ourselves for that day,' Max said, 'we have to know how you relate to people. Write your responses and read them out to each other. The group leader will observe and report to me. Not everyone will be chosen, so do your best.'

Sunless watched the large man from the group walk up to the stand and take some papers from the table. He returned and nodded to Sunless.

'We're one short, you'll do. Only kidding', and slapped him on the back. Sunless looked at the man's smile until it went away. 'Sorry about that,' the man said and pulled out a chair for Sunless.

'I'm here to find my father,' Sunless said.

The man smiled. 'That's great that you can just say it like that. I hear you. I wish I could come out and say it like that, wish I could spend another day with my dad.'

Sunless said, 'I'm picking him up this afternoon. But there's a lot of action outside, a lot of disturbances.'

The man stared at him a second. 'A lot of action, and we're in on it. That's great. Okay, everyone, let's begin, let's do this!'

The door seemed so far away to Sunless now, and yet another group had formed a circle of chairs between him and it, blocking his escape. If he didn't sit down he'd stand out. Nothing for it but to sit down in the group.

Max spoke again from the stand. 'Doctors are our best source for testing volunteers. You will remind them of the company's support in the past and introduce them to ways in which they can distribute our product.'

The group leader distributed sheets of paper and pencils. Sunless read the first instruction:

'Write the first three words that describe your people skills.'

Sunless wrote 'Avoid, Invisible, Watch'.

Fargoon must have retaken the stand because he spoke again, in a lower voice, a tone Sunless sometimes heard in lounge bars as singers were introduced: 'Remember, no one has to feel bad any more.'

'No one has to feel bad any more,' the woman in the group repeated.

Sunless looked at her page where she'd written in big letters, 'I am a people person. I like to listen to and understand people's concerns.' That was more than three words. Sunless even recounted them to make sure.

He read the next instruction on the paper: 'Write what you think of when you hear the word "negotiation".' That was easy. He wrote 'No', and then added, 'learning to say' before it so as not to appear harsh and stand out.

He then looked to his left, where the young man in the suit wrote, 'Negotiation is developing a win–win situation to get what you want in life.'

The woman covered up her answer because she wrote it with her elbow sticking out.

Sunless moved down to the next question: 'Write out a definition of disorders, then read the definition to your group members within sixty seconds of finishing.'

The woman wrote hers first and read it out in a sing-song voice: 'Disorders are when a person experiences a thing that they have not caused that makes them function wrong and stops them from being the person they can be.' She wiped away a tear and sniffled.

The group looked to Sunless, who brought his finger up to his eye to divert attention and read in a shaky voice, 'Disorders: when people don't obey orders.' He added, 'And that is a good thing.'

The woman pointed. 'Wait, that's unacceptable. You can't have those feelings. You need to develop other feelings. Affirmations like I will not feel angry today. I will feel the strength and light in me effusing out and changing the lives of others.' She stood, a large woman on two thin high heels, and spread her arms out. 'I am a person that loves and is loved and respected.'

On the other side of Sunless, the young man dropped his head like a hammer to his shoes.

'We are on a tight schedule,' Fargoon said from the stand. He wiped the rim and drank from a cup and gave a sign offstage and his image disappeared. Words and numbers flashed in rapid succession on the screen as the lights lowered.

The title shone white letters from the black screen: *JACK AND THE BEANSTALK*. The camera swung to a woman in a white coat who held a book up to the lens:

'Fairy tales can bridge the gap between Pharmalak and children with emotional conditions. Take this one, for example, a version of *Jack and the Beanstalk* from the eighteenth century:

'A poor widow lived with her only son, Jack, close to a forest. She grew ill and had to sell her cow. Jack knew that he had been a bad son and offered to sell it for her, but he sold the cow for beans instead of money. When she saw what Jack had done, she grabbed the beans and flung them into the garden, saying they were ruined for ever. Next morning, when Jack woke, he saw from his window that a beanstalk had grown high into the sky. Jack climbed it even though his mother told him not to, and he came to a strange country where a fairy appeared with a white wand in her hand and asked how he came to be there. When he told her he had climbed the beanstalk, she said, "Do you remember your father?" Jack said that he did not, that his mother would not tell him where his father was. "I knew your father," the fairy said, "and he was a good man who made friends with the Giant who came to live with him. One morning the Giant killed him, stole his possessions, and then evicted Jack and his mother." Pointing down a road, the fairy said, "The Giant lives that way." And she disappeared. Jack followed the road to a very large castle, where he hid in the oven and watched the Giant hold his favourite goose and shout "Lay!" and the goose laid a golden egg. Jack crept from the oven and stole the goose while the Giant slept.'

The woman in white closed the book and placed it in front of her.

'We already have enough to form a strategy,' she said. 'For instance, it's possible that Jack suffers from Pervasive Developmental Disorder, Oppositional Defiant Disorder and Conduct Disorder. Moreover, in failing to follow his mother's instructions, he shows signs of ADHD, or a simple attention-deficit disorder — that is, if he did not listen to her. If he deliberately ignored her, Oppositional Defiant Disorder cannot be ruled out.'

Jack's a brat, Sunless thought.

'Following that discussion, the parent might contact the company for information on medical products to address the child's difficulties', and then she stood to finish: 'Fairy tales make excellent copyright-free advertising material. Instant name recognition. *Jack and the Beanstalk*, brought to you by Pharmalak. After all, everyone trusts a fairy tale.'

Fargoon spoke as the film ended: 'One of our trainee doctors suggested a marketing campaign aimed at children to increase their awareness of our products. We thought this an excellent idea but did not anticipate the vociferous public reaction to the initial printing of one thousand books of the Pharmalak edition now recalled and recycled; however, I think we'll re-visit that opportunity in the future. In fact, I'm happy to announce that the new advertising campaign for Elevax has two phases. Phase one is about to begin, getting up to full steam in two weeks. Then, in about six months, we go national with a two-minute video advertisement. We're going to use the longer format saturation storytelling because people's attention spans aren't what they used to be. And we're going with *Jack and the Beanstalk*. Yes, the tale continues.'

People cheered.

'*Jack and the Beanstalk!*' someone said.

'And now I'll hand you back to Max. Max, please.'

Max's head replaced Fargoon's on the projector screen.

'Yes, what I want you all to do is write out and discuss possible endings for *Jack and the Beanstalk* and give the best ideas to the group leader who will forward them to me.'

The lights came back on. The room went quiet as people scribbled.

Sunless pretended to work and watched his group write furiously.

The woman said, 'I have an idea. Jack and the Giant meet on the ground floor and agree to have differences. The Giant retreats back up the beanstalk and Jack agrees to bring some eggs up to him every week. They agree to respect each other's boundaries and to discuss their issues, out in the open.'

She looked around for a response. Nobody made eye contact.

The young man then coughed and read what he'd written, that Jack and the Giant should agree to a division of monies and perform a mutual back-off to an agreed distance, then set up a fence or division line. No more exchanges, verbal or monetary, and no one trespasses on to the other's turf or area of control without total say-so from the other party; otherwise it's back to the axe and you can tear up any agreements.

Sunless looked at his blank page and said that Jack should

wait until the Giant was about a hundred feet from the ground and then chop down the beanstalk before he could reach the ground and do the same thing to Jack as he'd done to Jack's father.

The group leader nodded and noted down some of the comments.

The young man said, 'Why do we call them fairy tales anyway? Murder, jealousy, rage, why not human tales? The fairies would never have gotten up to a quarter of that stuff.'

The woman said, 'Everyone is equal, we owe it to our children, the children are our future, and everyone is different and unique.'

The young man closed his eyes.

Sunless said to the woman, 'I don't understand. Everyone is the same and everyone is different?'

'That's right,' the woman said. 'And why did you close your eyes when I was talking?' she said to the man.

'I do it sometimes,' he said, 'when I can't close my ears, because for some reason humans can't close their ears. We can close our eyes, mouths, hands, minds, but not these.' He pointed a finger to each side of his head.

'That's evolution,' Sunless said. 'If you can't hear what's coming, you'll have a short life.'

'I mean,' the young man said across the group to the woman, 'what has everyone being the same and different got to do with *Jack and the Beanstalk*, for the love of God?' He said to the group, 'I've been in her group all day and I'll have a short life if she doesn't shut the—'

'I knew it—' The woman gave a little bounce and turned on her seat. 'I took it as a disrespectful mannerism while I was talking about my life and my feelings. And I was right. You have disrespected my person.'

The young man pushed both hands out in front of him: 'Hey, lady—'

'My person and who I am!'

'Just stay on your side of the circle, got that? I'm not interested in your personal shit, you know what I mean?'

The group leader, a large man, rose to his full weight on his sandals and white cotton socks pulled up tight along his calves like cones. Then, as if forgetting what he wanted to say, he sat down again.

'Wait now, I'm hearing just a little,' said the group leader, raising his index finger, 'discord.' Pressing both palms down as if hoisting himself up from his chair, he smiled and said, 'Why don't we get with the programme here, okay? Let's get these questions done and move on to the next item on the agenda.' He shifted on the seat, hunched his shoulders and looked around the group. 'Okay? Are we okay on that? We need to focus here and not sweat the small stuff. Okay? We need to work together. Not lose the big picture.' He drew a large circle in the air with his hands.

'All I'm saying,' the woman said, 'is that we can have a society free of jealousy and anger and greed, then there'll be no need for fairy tales any more. A society without disorders, a perfect society based on mutual respect.' She sighed, 'And they're so violent anyway.'

'So we throw out the fairy tales,' the young man said.

The woman continued as if no one had said anything, 'No need for all that violence, especially when children are reading them. And fairy tales don't have a point, they're not practical. It would be better if we could discuss with the child the disorders as they happen in the story. Then at least we're not wasting time. As a parent, that's my duty to bring up my child well adjusted.'

Sunless said, 'I'd like to share another ending I have for *Jack and the Beanstalk*.'

'Yes, the young man said. 'Yes, please. Say something, please. Now.'

'What happens in my alternate ending is that Jack hides in the oven until the Giant eats his evening meal, calls for the goose that lays the golden eggs, and falls asleep. Jack crawls out of the oven and looks back and realizes the oven was very hot, and it's quite hot because someone turned it on. The wife of the giant betrayed him. Then the giant opens his eyes and says, "I smell the blood of angels." Jack gets away anyway. The rest is the same as before. Giant chases Jack, Jack cuts down beanstalk. Giant dies, Jack gets the eggs.'

'In a way,' the young man said, 'even though I have no idea what you're talking about, and I mean none whatso-ever, I prefer your version to the real thing.'

'What is the real thing?' Sunless said.

The man raised his hands and dropped them, looked at his watch, leaned back and sighed.

'We should respect all persons and cultures equally,' the woman said.

Fargoon spoke from the stand in his lounge voice: 'Doctors are a signature on a prescription, a necessary evil, some might say, though I would not, between our products and our customers. Our job is to bridge that gap and to reach the people. And now the second film, which illustrates some easy-to-remember scientific principles in relation to anxiety. It may inform your discussions with people. Roll the film, please.'

The room went black as the projector rolled and large red letters glowed starkly from the screen: *HYPOTHAL-AMUS, ORIGIN OF ANXIETY.*

The scene was a mountain pasture with a single bison standing in the middle. The bison did not move. The camera did not move. After a few seconds, a head rose above the tall grass, then an arm, then a spear. The camera zoomed into a woman wearing an animal skin as she rose to full height and pointed the spear; another person joined her, a man, also wearing an animal skin, and he, too, raised a spear. Sunless watched as both threw the spears into the bison, which remained perfectly still. Then people wearing different coloured animal skins appeared from behind boulders and chased off the first group before dragging the animal into the high grass.

A voice-over accompanied the rest of the short film, which included a scene where men fought with straw clubs, beating each other over the head until one fell down, clutching his forehead (where, Sunless observed, the man had not been struck). The voice was Fargoon's, speaking now over a light drumbeat:

'At Pharmalak, our focus on mental health is the hypo-thalamus, a cluster of cells in the ancient part of the brain that houses our primitive instincts, where we know fear originates. The hypothalamus is purely instinctive and acti-vates only to create a fight-or-flight decision until the danger subsides. Another ancient part of the brain, the amygdala, activates the hippocampus, a nearby cluster of neurons that learns dangerous situations. The amygdala sends a snapshot and says, "Remember this".'

The screen showed more images of men lighting fires

and dragging carcasses around the field. Fargoon's voice drifted in again:

'Even when the danger passes, sometimes the amygdala will continue to flood the brain with a primitive and powerful torrent of danger signals. Traces of fear persist after the danger has passed because, although the old part does its job and makes us frightened, the new, rational part of our brain can't let go of the fear, leading to anxiety. In lay terms, we want to get the ancient and modern parts of the brain talking to each other.'

Next they watched a short clip of two men on the ground, tugging at bones and cloth with their teeth and snarling at each other (one of whom, Sunless observed, was wearing a watch). Another scene showed three men and a woman sleeping on the floor of a cave around a feeble fire. Then some still photographs: black smoke rising from a cottage, an artillery piece pounding a tank turret in a wheat field, a torn man entwined in a parachute.

Fargoon spoke softly: 'Modern people are Stone Age people. The hypothalamus still sees adversaries and threats around every corner; it makes us fearful, but the modern brain can't turn the fear off. We trained these volunteers to activate the older part of the brain and hopefully a switch-off mechanism, and we will study them to see how they cope with anxiety in the future.'

The film ended and the screen went back to the projected image of Fargoon, who smiled. 'This is how you find the right chemical response to anxiety. I know of no drug company bold enough to undertake that experiment. Research trials, even something like Stone Age Tactical

Training, are the way we prove drugs, and all that science is what you're promoting.'

When the lights came back on, Max was standing at the microphone. 'Please form into three lines up to the railings here,' he said, 'to receive your samples and brochures.' The room rose and people formed three lines.

Sunless stood with them. It was getting hotter. Maybe the heat from the projector screen was doing it, combined with all these people crammed into a room. He stood straight like a cardboard dancing man, giving an occasional yelp to keep people away from him. That didn't deter the group leader, who smiled at him. 'I'm Rod, by the way. Isn't this great about the Amydagdala in the brain and all?'

The lines moved forward. Someone touched Sunless because he wasn't shuffling forward fast enough. Sunless yelped. Rod continued, as if he'd heard nothing. Sunless shuffled forward. The heat in the building. He wiped his neck.

Rod said, 'An exciting day for all of us, isn't it? I hear it cures neurosis of the liver, this new drug. I'm into EOW: Emotional Organ Work. Brand-new, scientifically studied therapy. I have my own practice, half conventional, half alternative. I have a PhD in psychology, actually. Yale, but I don't advertise that, don't want to intimidate people. This is a side-job for me. If I make enough here I can get a bigger office.'

They shuffled another step together. Sunless pretended he wore what horses did to keep things out of the sides of his eyes. Rod continued, 'And jealousy of the spleen. It may address that.'

'Isn't that where it is anyway?' someone else said from another line. 'In the spleen?'

'Actually, it's anger that's in the spleen,' Rod said. 'But I believe what lies in the spleen is a kind of craftiness.' He curved his hand.

Sunless wanted to move to another line but that would make him stand out. The heat was everywhere. He saw men loosen their shirts.

He said to Rod, 'You still think we're lining up for the new pill?'

'That's what we're doing, my friend.'

Sunless said, 'I went to mass one time; I think my father brought me when he was ill once. He was trying out some new ideas and didn't want to miss out on a cure.'

'Wise man.'

'And I saw the golden plate go around that people put money in, and the priest raise the host up, you know, the body?'

'The host – the body and blood of Christ?' Rod said.

'Yes, that,' Sunless said. 'I saw that it was really a pill he was holding up.'

Rod nodded. 'Oh, Mr Marx's dictum that religion is the opium of the people? That's old. Cliché City, my friend.'

'No, I mean it was a pill. The priest even said, "Take this and you'll feel better."'

'No, he didn't,' Rod said. 'He said, "Take this, it's the body" – you know I can't remember, but something like that.'

Sunless said, 'So I went to the altar and lined up and held the pill in my hands when it was dispensed to me and placed it in my pocket and brought it home, and I had that thing under a microscope in a second. The eyeball of Sunless on Jesus.'

Rod said, 'You put the body of Christ under a microscope?'

Sunless sensed a re-evaluation of his candidacy for company representative.

'The pill. Well, the thing was some kind of starchy bread, not a drop of blood in sight. Tasted it, didn't like the quality. I thought to myself, *I smell the blood of angels*. This is what an angel would taste like for definite.'

'Angels – what?' Rod was looking around him.

Sunless stepped toward the railings. 'Anyway, I wondered what was really in that pill to make everyone go back to their seats in the church and say the same thing. The only answer was that the angels were in the pills. The same angels with the same messages. A Trojan horse. You take the pill and they're in your bloodstream, taking over your system, making you believe things that aren't even there. Making you see things. You'll do anything if you take those pills, that's what I discovered. That's why it's such a valuable thing, gets held above a gold chalice, why it gets offered up to the ceiling.'

Rod did not move with Sunless but stayed a step behind.

Sunless said while looking forward, 'Anyway, I wrote to the priest: "I carried your pill home. I brought it home, examined it. No body in there unless it's pulverized into powder. Am keeping it in my house, in a glass container, waiting for them to make the break. And who are they, I hear you ask, as if you didn't know. Tell your angel friends I don't take angel pills. No obedience pills for Sunless."'

Rod said, 'You're admitting you sent an abusive and threatening letter to a priest?'

'Did you believe me?' Sunless said.

Rod faltered and laughed. 'You had me there. Good one.'

'And after I wrote the letter to the priest I kept a good watch on the glass container. I've stood watch a bunch of times, waiting for them to come out and talk. My questions are: who are you? Who do you represent? What happens exactly when the host is swallowed?'

Sunless looked behind him. Rod had dropped away into another line.

That was a pity, because Rod might have learned something about what happens when the health care industry and the government really start working together. He had it on good authority that in 1699, in some town in Italy, a few doctors figured out that tuberculosis was lots of invisible microbes that floated in the air between people, and they told the authorities. Wasn't long at all before the local magistrate comes out with a new law, and Sunless memorized it: 'Henceforth, the names of the deceased should be reported to the authorities and measures undertaken for disinfection.'

You can always trust the government to get involved. The doctors make a discovery, and because it involves information, the government is on to it before you can draw a breath. Report the names to the authorities. Yes, of course. And then when you have those names of the fellows who died, you get the names of their friends and family, their friends, and on top of that another list with their friends. Then the government goes house to house and starts asking questions. Doors get kicked in and more names get mentioned. One disease brings another: men in long coats looking for secrets you may or may not be keeping.

As these thoughts entered and left the head of Sunless, he observed something flit about the head of Fargoon up on the giant screen. Specifically, Sunless saw a dot bouncing on the screen behind Fargoon. Sunless focused, held his hand above his eyes to make sure. He nodded to himself. *Yes*, at last, here it was, this was it! The gathering, the order of the fly. Everyone pretending to be a fool. It all made sense now. So powerful you'd never notice it, like the real powers in the world. Under the radar screen. There it was, the real power in the building. Not a messenger, not a camera, but the fly itself, the thing itself, the seat of power in Pharmalak.

A fly bouncing around Fargoon's head.

And here Sunless was, shuffling in a line to the railings, to his induction into the order of the fly, then off to the woods for another ceremony, probably. Plans for distribution of the drug. Wearing of special cloth and repetition of oaths, secret handshakes and codes. Direct line to the president of the country. Division of sectors. More converts. Conventions in lots of major cities with major psychiatric organizations. The American Organization of Psychiatrists. Respected doctors with bow ties lending their names to published scientific studies they may not have even read. Everyone making a ton of money and not a damn thing to be done about it.

But he wasn't afraid now. Sunless had seen the fly.

He reached the top of the line, took a bag from the

person at the top, at the railings, a blue plastic bag, with a logo that depicted the monolith of Pharmalak rising from a rock, and above it a light, and above that, a pair of giant wings circling a globe, with P on one side and L on the other, and to Sunless the globe was an eyeball.

'And now,' Fargoon said, 'I am pleased to show you the phase one advertisement. Play the video, please.'

The screen changed again to a video of a woman arranging flowers by a window with a swing set on the lawn in the background. She looked worried. It was raining. Smooth violin music ushered in a slogan that slowly materialized on the screen: 'Elevax, The Answer to Anxiety.' The woman smiled widely and the violin was joined by an orchestra. The sun emerged from the clouds.

Murmurs. The audience clapped. 'Yes,' someone said. Even louder claps.

Excellent, Sunless thought. Bright prospects for everyone. You can take the man from the Stone Age but you can't take the Stone Age from the man.

The heat had become unbearable. Sunless sweated openly. Even though the questionnaires had been taken up, the woman had not handed up hers. She sat on her seat, eyes closed, smiling. Sunless read what she'd written in large letters above her name on the top of the first page: 'I believe in everyone's potential. No one is to blame for what happens in life. This is America. Love it or leave it!!!!'

Meanwhile, Fargoon was acknowledging the applause and stood with his arms folded, nodding happily. Then he held his arms up for silence.

'Since Christmas is upon us, or the holidays as they say these days, I wanted to move the proceedings to a close in a somewhat lighter vein. The next and final clip you are about to see records the efforts of a Revd. Marlin Fenster, a man we brought here last year. Revd. Fenster is a man of deep Christian principles, a member of the charismatic movement in Georgia, who had embraced alternative health care philosophies and incorporated them into his motivational speeches.'

A laugh from the audience.

Fargoon raised a hand for silence and continued. 'Marlin Fenster contacted us with a request that we provide a setting – as it turns out, this very lecture hall – in which he could demonstrate one of his ideas for decreasing anxiety and promoting a positive outlook. A most interesting man, a most intense man. His idea is that if people laugh enough, it'll bring on happiness. We agreed, as his testimonials were excellent, on the condition that there were no religious references, and we invited a hundred members of the senior population of Park City to the event. It was a Saturday evening, as I recall. The film, please.'

The lecture hall went dark and the numbers counted down to one and then the title, *ANXIETY – THERAPIES – THE MARLIN FENSTER SHOW*.

A balcony, a party of four sitting with cocktails. The camera panned Park City. Sunset in the background, red haze, everyone smiling. Music from inside the condo. A glass door opened and an orange curtain billowed out to a woman holding a golf stick and a book. She sat on a deck chair and lit a cigarette, blew it at the sky, and smiled at the camera, looking happy and bored at the same time.

The scene cut to a jerky video from the lecture hall where two people paced up and down on the stage, holding signs:

'Laugh it away!'

'Try laughing!'

In the film the crowd clapped out of sequence, then the clapping quickened into applause and into cheers. A rising voice through loudspeakers said, 'And now, Marlin Fenster!'

A tanned man in a large white suit walked out into the circle of light on the stage and waved as his teeth shone in the spotlights. The voice in the loudspeaker said, 'Laugh! Laugh!'

The people in front of the camera laughed. Fenster paced the stage, waving and stomping.

'Laugh, laugh!'

His assistants worked the aisles, tapping the shoulders of those not laughing; they pointed at others and worked their way through the lines to get to them; they stood over the silent ones until they laughed too; they slapped the backs of those who laughed the best, whose shoulders heaved with laughing, and they pointed to them and clapped, to show everyone else that those people were doing the right thing.

'Laugh! Laugh!' Fenster yelled.

Soon every face on every line of seats seemed to break into a laugh. Some cheeks were wet with tears, other people held hands with the next person.

Fenster raised a hand, his assistants put fingers to their lips, and the laughing stopped. A few in the audience had to be tapped on the shoulder. One man in the fourth row had to be shaken, but he kept laughing until he was escorted out. Fenster pointed to him.

'Got carried away there, didn't we? That's okay, just laugh it away.'

A few clapped.

Fenster raised both arms. 'What did I say?' Then he put a hand to his ear and leaned forward.

'That's okay,' a few said.

'What? I can't hear you?'

'That's okay, just laugh it away.'

'Again!' he yelled.

'That's okay, just laugh it away.' Some clapped in time with the slogan.

An organ from somewhere behind the stage or maybe from the loudspeakers played a chord, and Fenster tapped a silver stick on the stage in time with the words. The slogan repeated every three or four seconds. Couples got to their feet and swayed in time. Fenster walked to the center of the stage and a single light shone on his bowed head. The arena went silent. A woman walked on stage flanked by two of Fenster's assistants.

'Your name?' he said.

'Sara.'

'Sara, I have a question for you. How do you feel tonight?"

Sara looked directly into the spotlight.

'I feel good.'

Fenster's face again, to her left. 'But Sara, I want to know this. I want to know if good is good enough?'

Sara laughed. 'Not for me. I want happy.'

Fenster nodded and tapped the stick until the audience caught the rhythm. 'Not for me. I want happy.'

The crowd roared 'happy'. Fenster raised his stick. All the lights came back on. The assistants ran to the stage and picked up new signs: 'Had a laugh lately?'

Fenster shouted, 'Well, have you?' He cocked his head for an answer.

'Yes,' a few shouted back.

The spotlights crisscrossed. Every face opened in a laugh. Men and women arched their backs, some rubbed their hands in their hair and some slapped their thighs.

The lights faded again to Fenster's face, lit centre stage by a single spotlight that panned right to a man beside him.

'Your name,' Fenster said.

'Tom.'

'Well, Tom, how are things for you?'

Tom spoke into the light: 'I feel pretty happy.'

The crowd cheered.

'Good man, Tom. Thank you, Tom.' And Tom moved out of the light, which expanded to include all of Marlin Fenster.

'And now,' Fenster said. 'Tom's wife!' The lights drew down on a woman who walked onstage from the side.

Fenster said, 'And are you happy tonight?'

The woman said nothing. Fenster seemed unsure what to do, but he kept his wide smile. The assistants stopped in their tracks.

The crowd waited. The husband waited. Fenster winked at the crowd. 'She's playing with us, I can tell.'

The husband put his arm on her shoulder and hugged her. 'Answer Mr Fenster, darling.'

Fenster shook his head and spoke through his white smile, 'Let her answer.'

The woman coughed. 'I miss my old house. I don't like this place. I'm lonely here.'

Someone gasped. Fenster swung to the husband and said, 'What is this?'

'I don't know, she's not happy in Park City. Maybe we should have stayed in Iowa near our grandchildren.'

Fenster kept up the smile. He thrust his arms out and faced the crowd.

'Not happy – well, what can we do about that?'

No one answered. His smile faltered. Fenster looked around him and said again, 'What can we do about that?'

The woman sobbed in the silence that followed Fenster's question. Her husband held her.

Again Fenster said, 'What can we do?' He walked to an assistant and whispered something through his white teeth. The assistant sang, with a wobble in his voice, 'That's okay, just laugh it away.'

'That's right!' Fenster said. 'Now everyone!'

Fenster's assistants worked the aisles again. One by one, the lines of seats joined the laughter. Images of laughing people.

'Laugh! Laugh!' Fenster shouted.

Then there seemed to be a cut in the film. The camera swung to the doors. People streaming out to their golf carts. No one talked much, except about the drop in temperature; the cocktail hour in someone's condo, the tennis game for the next morning.

The film ended. Fargoon coughed. 'That is an example of how easily a corporation can become involved in questionable practices.'

Sunless watched the blank screen for a minute. The possibilities were endless. Not a one-time show as Fargoon said, but a weekly, even daily therapy forced on old people by a powerful company, day after day, herded in and all laughing on cue. He thought about infiltrating a future session of the *Marlin Fenster Show*, but then he realized the horror of being filmed and having to laugh for extended periods in order to remain anonymous.

And he knew what he had to do.

He knew because a great power structure falls easily. It's the small ones you can't dislodge. The local councillor, the mayor of a small town. Want to get rid of them? Good luck. But the bigger ones go easier if you find the switch. The whole structure comes down. The Celtic warrior Brennus, after winning a fight with a few Roman armies in Italy, walked into the empty city of Rome and didn't know what to do with it, so he left. The Khan's Mongol armies turned back from the gates of Europe in 1241, having defeated everyone sent out to meet them. All they had to do was march a couple of weeks to the shores of the Atlantic Ocean and Christianity was dead. They went back home. And now here was he, Sunless, within fifty feet of the fly. He knew what to do, unlike Brennus and the Mongols. Oh yes. Here comes Sunless!

He threw the bag and it sailed over the group in slow motion, and everyone ducked as the pills, brochures, coupons and summarized study results sprayed like shot. He swung the bag again though it was empty now and his face twisted like wrung plastic. He lifted the bag of samples from the woman's chair and headed for the screen. There it was, bobbing. Then he turned in mid-step because the fly was, of course, at the projector itself, probably reviewing slides and videos before they were shown. Good tactic that, sending him the wrong way. He headed for the projector and raised the bag over his head and said, 'Give me back my dad, you son of a bitch', and he brought the bag down and the room went black and no one moved. Just this silence, like after a train wreck. Then one shout. Then two. Someone said to switch on the lights. Sunless checked the bag. Right in the centre of the globe on the plastic bag, a red streak. And on the projector's glass plate, a wing, crushed.

'Got you,' Sunless said. 'At long last I got you.'

Someone screamed, a high scream.

Sunless looked to where people were pointing.

On the screen Fargoon's giant head said, 'And this is the start of a new day in mental health care.' He said it with blood blotched on his cheek and mouth.

SUNLESS 8

Thankfully no one switched on the lights and Sunless did a runner. He weaved unnoticed under the red EXIT sign and scattered down the hall and ran across the lobby and into the café.

He checked his watch. He was a few minutes early but needed the time to regroup. Spread out among the tables, doctors, nurses, men in suits, newspapers, eating, drinking. Immediately to his right, a politician Sunless had often seen on television sat under a television with what looked like company executives, judging by the brochures they showed him. The politician nodded in approval and cut through the apple cake with a fork as a young man pointed to some figures in the brochure and put his case.

'I agree in principle,' the politician said, 'that your industry in general needs protection for patents and more aggressive federal funding for research.'

Sunless glanced above them at a commercial on the television screen that showed an old person walking in a circle in her living room.

Constantly forgetful? Can't remember where you left the car keys, your wallet, or even what day of the week it is? You may be suffering from Accelerated

Memory Deficiency Syndrome, or AMDS. Now there is a new product, Nemocot, that delays the onset of AMDS. Don't wait. Talk to your doctor about Nemocot.'

He saw the three girls from the train talking, bent over cups in the corner, and he kept to the outside as he passed the tables, pretending to read notices on the wall, and poured himself a coffee from the self-serve counter before sitting behind them, his face still turned away. They must have been taking part in drug evaluations, like him.

The girls were loud as they discussed school.

'I'm taking a test on some play, haven't read it, need to learn some quotes,' the girl in leather said.

'What's the play?' the small one said.

'*Hamlet*. It's a tragedy by, by Shakespeare.'

The small one opened both palms in the air: 'I hate that, when they make me read stuff that has absolutely nothing, nothing to do with me and my life.'

'It's unbelievable. But I need some quotes. Otherwise I have to look it up on the web.'

The girl in blue raised a finger. '"To be, or not to be. That is the question.' That's a quote from *Hamlet*.' She beamed.

The leather one said, '"To be or not, that's a question." Now I need another one, because we need at least two for the test.'

The girl in blue shrugged. 'That's all I know.'

'That's great. That's just great. Now I have to do a *Hamlet* search and then get a quote.'

'Wait, you can try a Shakespeare search and then do quotes. *Hamlet* is always in there, near the top, because you've got a bunch of students doing the same search every day. Grab one and you're done.'

'Great.'

'Anyway,' the blue one said, 'I did a Celexa search this morning before I caught the train. My mother got some prescribed and took one yesterday morning with another drug and she was high all day.'

'Interesting.'

'So I checked the bottle. Generic name is Citalopram. And I'm wondering—'

'Citalopram. That's a chemical class for depression?'

'Yeah, but I wonder what they interacted with to give her that high, what else she used that day.'

'Did you find it?'

'No. I went through the entire medicine cabinet, but she'd got so many medicines that I couldn't tell. Zoloft or Zyban, it could have been one of those two. Or maybe Xanax.'

'The generic name for Xanax is Alprazolam. Definitely.'

Leather said, 'I think I'm bipolar with mild OCD and latent anorexia. I need to find out exactly what's wrong with me. Get a diagnosis and move on. You have to keep the pressure on doctors, don't let them slack off. You have to know your terms.'

Blue said, 'Last year I thought I had Borderline Personality Disorder.'

'That was last year's thing,' the small one said. 'That went out last year. Nobody has that now.'

'Hey, so what was that quote again by the playwright guy?'

Sunless watched a woman in a nurse's uniform put her

plate on the dishwasher counter and leave the café. One of the doctors moved near his shoulder. 'Do you mind?' Sunless left the self-serve counter with a pair of irritated eyeballs stuck to the back of his head. Sometimes when he was at home he stood for minutes or longer staring at the television or a door, deep in thought or no thought at all, sometimes in front of the refrigerator, one hand on the open door, just standing there looking into the light and the rows of food, imagining that the food was a city or simply looking at the labels or one letter on a label.

On the wall a large white map showed the various rooms and floors of the hospital complex. Sunless located the café and traced a route downstairs to where his father might be.

He sat at a table with his coffee. He heard one of the girls lower her voice, which is why he noticed it.

'That's him, that's the nut who attacked us in the train.'

And it happened that everyone, *everyone*, stopped talking as the girls said the word 'attacked'.

'Yes, that's the man who went nuts on the train and attacked us with a book.'

Sunless sighed. Any moment now, the orderlies will walk in after him with a stretcher and a syringe. Where was Jane? Was the café a trap? If the girls came at him they'd be taking pieces of a coffee cup out of their faces for a month. He'd had quite enough. Yes, enough, enough, enough and more enough on top of that, that's when you know you have enough, when the enoughs keep coming with no stops between them.

And while he was at it, he made a note to tell Fargoon when he saw him next that Pharmalak had it all wrong. To explain why Pharmalak had it all wrong, he'd need a tissue and a pen. He got up and took a tissue from the coffee stand and since he didn't have a pen, he wrote with a pen he made out of the words that came into his head:

Why Pharmalak has it all wrong. You didn't need to pay people all that money to come up with names for drugs. You could come up with memorable names without having to be so creative. Let's see, the new marketing strategy: call drugs by the disease or disorder they address. Sadness, Anxiety, Anger, Panic Attack, Rage. It could get complicated when the pharmaceutical industry discovered more disorders. Going into a pharmacy and asking for a bottle of Generalized Social Anxiety Manic Obsessive-Compulsive Disorder medication could turn out to be a mouthful – if you coughed you'd have to start all over again, but that could all be figured out later, maybe use an acronym – could be as simple as saying 'I need GSAMOCD medication', something fast off the tongue. So let's call drugs after what they do, instead of coming up with names, and for updates, place a simple number after each name. If someone suffers from rage, for instance, you could call a drug Rage-15 as opposed to a different company's Rage-12, and Sad-56 as distinct from Sad-5, an earlier medication.

He imagined the career woman with her prescriptions at the pharmacy:

'Yes, I'll have ten Obsessive-Compulsive Disorder pills, please. Give me a couple of rage and fear capsules. And listen, a month of those denial tablets while you're at it.'

'Do you have a prescription for the denials?'

'Hang on, checking. Yes, yes, here it is. Denial. Thirty ten milligram pills, one per day.'

'That's a lot. You must be in severe denial.'

'That's actually not true, and you know it.'

Sunless thought how much more straightforward the commercials would be: 'Do you suffer from rage? Do you scream at people for no good reason? Are you an angry person? Make enemies more than most? If so, ask your doctor about Rage-17 and Anger-4, and while you're there, mention Obsessive-3 and Jealous-77, since you probably suffer from those conditions too.'

Sunless patted himself on the back. Now that's a commercial message.

So you end up selling drugs like Anxiety-1. What else is there? He decided to take two existing names and cut them in half and then join them. Xanloft? Paxloft? Yes, *Paxloft*.

For those demanding researchers he would justify it thus in a written report: write the name Zoloft in black ink, place it under a microscope and examine the properties of the letters. 'Zo' sounds like 'so', and 'loft' is like 'lofty' or 'high', which leaves you with 'so high'. Next put Paxil under the scope. 'Pax' is the Latin for 'peace' and 'il' sounds like 'ful', which give you 'peaceful'. Then cut both pills in half and join them with your spit into a single product with the name Paxloft, 'peace high', or 'a piece of high'.

Try saying this: 'Take two Paxlofts and call me in the morning. Brand new medicine. Good results so far.' A bit difficult to pronounce but it had a ring to it all the same.

Then he thought some more. Why restrict the campaign to television and posters around town? Take it straight to the people. Have doctors go to corporations with little suitcases full of prescription pads and medication. Dr Sunless, physician to the executive branch. Hang around cafés where the stockbrokers go, Excuse me, I'd like to interest you in a new product, Greed-1. It's got a little pep in it as well to help you stay up late, catch the foreign markets opening, and you'll still be at your desk at breakfast when the losers come to work. Or bump into a car dealer at his favourite bar. I'm sorry, I didn't notice you standing there. You could do with a bit of charisma. Sales low this week? Try this. Yes, what an effective way to sell medicine. And not a new approach at all, so there'd be no persuading board members about this marketing strategy. All you'd have to say is, 'Time to go back to the old ways.' What old ways, you might be asked.

You would say that once upon a time there were the 1800s, and the 1800s were happening in the Midwest, and at that time there you had the movers and shakers, the families living on the edge of civilization who saw nothing but wheat fields and mountains when they looked out of the window in the morning, and women who saw nothing but children all the live-long day, and these movers and shakers lived in small farmhouses, and at that time the disease that killed most was the distance to the doctor. But you had to be there, digging up a country to make it new. And the drug for the 1800s set was laudanum, that dark brown bottle. Laudanum, a curiously effective patent medicine sold at circuses, at crossroads, at your doorstep; here's a couple for you, madam. And how are the children? And how is the farm? And I have another one in my waistcoat pocket. Laudanum, laudanum, a little bit of morphine, that's all it is, well a lot of morphine, mostly morphine, but this is the thing: your children will sleep well, your worries will disappear, the future will brighten, that bad knee will work like new, your eyes will clear up, and that sore throat — what sore throat? Laudanum, laudanum, a patent medicine for general relief of the long list of what ails you. Arthritis, cough, vision troubles, bad back, pain in the extremities, pain in other areas, numbness, tingling, shortness of breath, lugubriousness, sloth, disturbances of the brain, the spine, and all nervous conditions.

Sunless imagined wheeling his cart into the lunchroom in the Town Hall at lunchtime. Sunless has laudanum! One bottle for ten bucks, two for eighteen. I hold the office of laudanum! *Laudanum, laudanum.* Bring a smile to your face and finish the race. *Laudanum, laudanum.* We're selling a lot of 'em. And how is your new job in the city? Stressful, of course. Talk to your doctor. Talk to your doctor about laudanum. Have you talked to your doctor about laudanum?

He smelled some perfume sit beside him, ever so slightly. 'Hi, I'm Jane,' she said.

SUNLESS 9

'Have you talked to Mr Fargoon today?' the perfume said again until Sunless looked up and saw the woman from the fairy tale video and saw something move in her hand, a vase with red and blue trim, might be nice in the window with a flower big enough to block out the sunlight but also add some brightness to the room with its own colour. That's what Sunless thought, but briefly, since he wanted to keep most of his thoughts free.

'I know who you are.'

'Yes, we met about six months ago, right here, in fact.'

'And you must be Paul's son then?'

'I am.'

'Can you follow me, please?'

He followed her down the stairs into a basement area until they reached a sign, Mortuary Services, where she opened a door and they entered a steel room: steel counters, steel gurney, steel instruments, steel floor, all steel, a planet of shiny grey steel, awash in antiseptic.

So this was the room, the secret room that Sunless knew must be here, the laboratory that kept his dad from the grave. Jane stood on the other side of the gurney. She smiled.

'This is where he was,' she said. 'Your father.' She placed

her hands on the gurney. 'Your father lay here, while he was with us. Some people like to place their hands here.'

Sunless stepped back and searched around the room at eyelevel, at charts of the human anatomy, bones, tissue, organs, revealed at different levels. A light hung low over the metal dissecting table that itself slanted to a catch basin, a drain and a faucet. Tongs, cutting instruments. Doctors manoeuvring long, spiny sutures with needles. Steel scrubbed into again and again. Yet something cut into the antiseptic.

Her perfume.

Barely noticeable. Sunless thought wearing perfume must be the art of being a ghost, just enough so that it wasn't quite present, not entirely absent. She herself seemed a bit like a ghost to him then, in her white coat, and layered above that, her black hair, and another layer, this time her face, painted over her body and set in place. And when her mouth moved to speak, another layer emerged from her, this time of sound and words, though they didn't match up fully in sequence. He thought that if he touched her his finger would go through her like water and she would shimmer. Maybe he wasn't in a mortuary at all, maybe he was standing by a lake.

Instead, she touched Sunless. She must have moved like a ghost too – he never saw her coming around the gurney.

'You seem like such a contained person, Sunless. Do you mind me saying that?'

He said, ' Is there anything left at all?'

'There are some remains,' Jane said. 'And we left his heart.' She held his gaze until he looked again at the gurney.

Sunless saw the scissors in a tray of the dissection table, the knives cutting his father into his parts, an incision at the head and from the neck down along the thorax and opening it out like flaps, revealing a heart, the lungs, the kidneys, examining the pieces of a man, a man in pieces. His father must have become unrecognizable after that first cut. Was the person still his father even?

She said, 'We organized a memorial service for your father last week — all the medical students at the hospital attended. It was a wonderful service, and we celebrated what your father gave us and the medical community, what he gave to those he never met.'

'You held a service for him?'

She nodded and moved to the door. She thought a moment as if searching for the right words: 'You've been coping very well.'

He heard her say *copying*. 'There's a reason,' he said, 'why womb and tomb rhyme—'

'What?' she said.

Sunless said, 'I can't stay here, I have to go, I have to go.'

'I have your father's ashes here with me, in this urn,' she said and placed the vase on the gurney. Sunless looked at the red and blue trim. It was clearly a vase, not an urn.

'This is it?' he said.

'Yes, five pounds of white ash, from your father's bones. We cremated the remains this afternoon. We couldn't find you, and we presumed you didn't want to attend.'

'I felt the heat and saw the flames in the sky,' Sunless said, 'and wondered what they were. Now I know.'

'Really — I didn't see you in the crematorium. Were you there?'

'No, outside, but I saw the man from the bar – was he helping you?'

'What man from what bar?' Jane said.

Sunless looked inside the vase. 'What is this powder?'

'It's the ash from his bones. I can describe the process if you wish. The temperatures, the cooling tray. Some people tell me they want to understand the process of cremation.'

Sunless shook his head. 'What is there to know? All I know is there was a fire, because I saw it,' he said. 'And I thought the end of the world had come.'

She looked puzzled.

'Never mind,' Sunless said, picking up the vase.

'The end of the world?' she said?

'Getting him back, same thing as the end.'

Jane wanted to leave, he could sense it. Twitchy, fidgeting. 'We did send you a letter advising you that his body would be ready today. The staff goes on Christmas vacation tomorrow, and that we'd arranged for a service this evening in Salt Lake Cemetery. Seven o'clock. We're taking care of the arrangements, of course. And we retained some of his remains for the service.'

'Seven o'clock?' Sunless said.

'Didn't you get the letter?'

'What letter?'

She said, 'I hand-delivered it myself on Saturday. I was going past your house anyway. I knocked and then I tried calling your name.'

'I didn't check my letterbox. What did you say?'

'I called your name through the letterbox slot.'

Sunless turned to her. 'Nothing else?

'Nothing.'

'It's strange,' Sunless said.

'It must be, I know,' she said, 'being here.'

'I don't know, ask him.'

Sunless stared at the vase and smelled the perfume as it left and as it said something about coming back any time he felt he needed to. The vase fit entirely in his hand, weighed five pounds. But he had his father back. You got his body, I get his ashes.

Yes, of course I'll come back.

Sunless 10

Sunless left Mortuary Services and walked back to the café, which had thinned out, people gone for the weekend and then Christmas, and it would be the New Year before most of them came back. A few doctors drank coffee. Although the place was almost empty, the television was still broadcasting a programme about Chronic Maladjustment Syndrome, still under investigation, not an official disorder yet, but some causes for concern were being raised in the medical community; leading experts in the field were pointing to a disturbing new trend in urban children. Preliminary research indicated that Nemocot—

He left the building, out past the sliding glass doors and into the chill of Park City. Someone said the train from Salt Lake City was delayed half an hour because of snow on the tracks. It was very quiet, a snowy silence, a few people walking the platform, so he walked into town with the vase in his hands. The smell reached him from the huge pine tree at the other end of the street, the crunch of feet on the snowy pavements dug into his eardrums, and the Christmas decorations swinging on wires overhead draped themselves across his eyes; on the opposite side of the street the warm lights of a bookstore glowed orange on to the snow outside, and inside, near the entrance, a woman read in a chair, a children's book, he could tell by the cover; a bird flew over the roof of the store, no, two birds. The wind blew the flakes across the town, filling up the windows and the doorways. A face loomed and went by, another 'Happy Christmas!'

'Yes,' Sunless said.

'Happy Christmas,' he said when the person was safely gone. No one noticed. No one said a thing. Nothing came from the sky. It was what it was: snowing, and if Sunless hadn't been clutching his father's ashes in his hands at that moment he would have sworn it was snowing his father's pulverized bones down across the mountainside.

He was coming down.

He had no friends. He had no anybody. He did not know what he was going to do with the rest of his life, as brief as it was going to be, and how brief. And he had only a thin jacket to wear against the cold. Sunless held the vase in front of him to block out some of the wind that emptied the sky clear, as if the snowstorm were figuring out whether to stay or go. As he reached the platform the flakes gave way to a clear night that blew some clouds across the stars. The train pulled in and Sunless waited until everyone had boarded, then chose a nearly empty carriage, though he saw the girls in the front as he entered. They didn't see him, and he walked quietly to the rear and sat by a window, watching Pharmalak slide out of view and the white slopes rise and fall in the dark.

The train tilted down the mountain, and he was riding down that mountain in the dark, with his dad, what was left of him. Sunless wondered what he really knew about his father, what anyone does. He made a mental list of the things he had observed about him. Sunless knew how he dressed, where he worked, his name, the words his father tended to use more than others, the ways he was kind and happy and angry and fed up and how sometimes he was none of those things. Sunless knew what his father believed and did not believe, what he liked to eat and watch on television.

At Kimball Junction the girls filed out silently.

As the train picked up speed again Sunless took a page from his pants pocket and unwrinkled it, brushed some salt crystals from the writing and slanted it up to the interior lights:

The Egyptians built pyramids that made clocks out of the sky. Their kings lay in state, surrounded by drawings on the walls, pictures of hunting, of contests, of balmy days by the Nile. *This is what we did in life*. The Celts heaved giant boulders that stand in the western islands today. We don't know what they did and said around those stones when they came to bury their brothers and sisters, fathers and mothers, their friends.

In Queen Victoria's coffin: her wedding veil and her mourning cap for Prince Albert, who had died thirty-nine years before her; over a layer of charcoal, Albert's dressing gown, Albert's cloak, a plaster cast of his hand; on top of these items a cushion, and on top of that, the queen's body, in whose hand was placed a picture of John Brown, covered with flowers.

What you will find at graves: books wrapped in

plastic, name pins, photographs and portraits; people stooped over, a knee touching the ground, a forehead the hand, prayers and poems for friends, for wives, for sons, for babies; drawings from children for their mothers to see.

When a waterfowl dies, her mate will call again and again for her, returning to the places they shared: the water in the upturned trash-can lid, the clay between rocks where they fed on seeds, the rushes in which they slept on summer nights.

After Shah Jahan married Mumtaz Mahal in 1612 she bore him fourteen children and died in 1630, aged thirty-nine. The Emperor went behind closed doors for a week and reappeared with white hair. He ordered twenty thousand craftsmen to build a mausoleum taking seventeen years. Even now, after hundreds of years, its façade suggests a silk veil covering a face. The Taj Mahal preserves a great sorrow. You stand before it and think that even a gentle breeze might move the stone walls, like linen drying on a line.

Sunless watched the yellow blanket of Salt Lake City appear below him as the train arrived at the point just above the valley. It had snowed there, too, snow on the temple, on the town square, on the houses along the foothills, the wide straight streets that ran west to the great desert. The moon was rising above Antelope Island, itself curved over the lake, and west of that, the endless white salt he could not yet see. Sunless pressed his face to the glass until the face on the other side met his exactly.

He could feel it. He was coming down.

As the train levelled off at the bottom of the valley Sunless thought of Fargoon sitting alone in his office after the lecture and writing at his desk with pills falling out of his pockets, streaming out of his nose and mouth, like the tale of the porridge that would not stop pouring out of the pot. The pills swarm across the desk. They pile to the edge and spill off on all sides and cloud the floor, inching up the sides of the walls. Tons of pills spill out into the corridor outside his office, along the corridor, into the foyer, fill up the glass, fill up the lecture halls, the waiting rooms, spray out of the doors and down the street, covering Park City, the trees, and then come the first news reports of rising yellow pills up the mountainside, scraping the sky until a lid snaps shut, and it's night, and all the pills are resting for the day. But when you turn on the television, the pills are there talking about the news, and they hand over to more pills that talk about the news, and the first pills say thank you for the news, and now this important message.

The train arrived at his stop. Sunless waited until the last moment before running out the doors and then proceeded to walk the street in his white shirt, holding the vase in front of him at face level and at arm's length to avoid easy detection. When he arrived at his street he waited at the corner of the block for a couple of minutes to see if anyone was waiting outside his house. He checked the ground for footprints or tyre tracks. When it was safe to do so, he slipped into the alley and entered by the back door. The television blared from the living room as Sunless detached the dancing man from the window and put it back in the closet. Wasting no time, he ran to his bedroom window and searched outside for unusual activity.

Nothing out there in the salt desert. I don't buy it, Sunless thought. Something else is going on with that brother of mine. He'd have made this trip today but for something else that's bothering him. Oh, if you weren't my brother I'd be watching you, watching you so very carefully, Salt. And you should be watching me. I've tried not to let you see me.

Sunless left his father's ashes on the windowsill and, even though it was dark now, searched for a face reflected in the window, the face of his brother who looked out so many nights to the lake, wondering where all the people he had lost were gone. Then Sunless used his binoculars to scan the mountainside while listening for loud footsteps. Yes, Jack was done with the Giant, but the Giant probably wasn't done with Jack; therefore Jack might have to make a return trip up the mountain with his axe. He had something more to discuss with Matthew Fargoon.

Salt

Salt 1

When I was young, the sun always shone blue on the shallow waters of the Great Salt Lake, less than a half mile from the house where we lived, and every few mornings in the summer my father and mother brought me to the shore for walks, and when I was nearly five years old, my mother's belly grew and then kept growing past the beginning of summer, until one evening in July my father stuck his head into my bedroom and asked if I wanted to go to the lake because he had a ship to launch. He held up a twisted trunk of wood that covered his face. 'A ship,' he said.

'But it's only a piece of timber,' I said. 'That's not a ship, Daddy.'

He put it in a bag. 'Wait, you'll see. Come on.'

And then we drove to the lake. When we got there my mother carried the blanket from the car and put it on the grass. My father carried a jug of coffee and I lifted a plate of biscuits, and we all sat down by the shore and watched the sun move lower and the lights of the city grow brighter in the east.

Then he stood and rolled up his pant legs. 'What do you think?' he said to my mother.

'Yes, it's time,' she said.

'Okay, we're going in,' he said and rattled the bag at me

with a smile. We all waded out a few yards into the warm
water, and he reached into the bag and took out the branch
and set it on the water and placed ten tea lights across it.
My mother lit them with matches.

'What's the name of the ship?' I said.

'No name yet,' she said.

We stood together and pushed the timber so it floated out
further. The evening sun made my father's skin like copper in
his white shirt. He hoisted me up on his shoulders, and I felt
how strong they were, how his face smelled of rum lotion. I
rubbed and pulled at his bristles and he laughed and danced
up to his knees in the water; I clung to him and closed my
eyes and could not smell enough of the salt, the cigarette
smoke off his shirt, the sweat running down his aftershave.

My mother walked to the floating timber and lay on her
back with her clothes on and floated, holding her belly
above the water. My father stopped jumping around and let
me down slowly and then he watched her very closely and
held my hand as we waded over to where she lay. The
timber touched her arm and bobbed. She pointed to it
and said to him,

'Look, Paul, our baby's first voyage.'

The timber tipped against her belly as a small wind flut-
tered the lights, but they all somehow stayed lit. My father
lay down in the water beside her and for a moment I did
not know what to do until she raised her hand and waited
until I put mine in hers.

'Come here, Salt.'

And we lay there in the shallow warm water of the lake.
She floated holding her belly above the water and smiled
when my father splashed her. The salt, she shouted. The

sun kept itself in the sky for as long as it could until it touched the lake too, and the flames of the tea lights lit our skin, then the water, and soon the night itself.

In August my father cleared out the spare room by filling the closets with the coats and books and everything else in that room that had been on the floor. Next day he painted the walls, and the day after that I walked in and saw a crib in the corner, the crib I lived in when I was a baby, and I wondered why someone was coming to visit for that long. My mother brought me shopping with her for clothes a couple of times, bags of them she piled into the car, and soon after when we got back to the house she'd flap the clothes open, lifting them above her head and looking them up and down. I saw her smile and thought I heard her talking to the clothes, which was unusual because there was nobody in them. She saw me and smiled again.

'You were once this small,' she said. I saw her face, through the thin blue blouse. She laid the new clothes on the kitchen counter near a vase of flowers and folded them again and put them flat on her bed. My father came home and attached a string with angels hanging off it across the top of the crib. I wanted to ask who was coming, but my parents were so happy I decided not to ask for now, because everyone seemed to know what was going on. Sometimes my mother seemed less happy when her belly grew bigger, sometimes very happy.

The next morning we went to the lake again and lay in the water again. My mother said, 'Salt, you'll have a brother soon.'

I lay on my back and looked at the clouds in the sky.

'When is he coming?' I said.

'In a few weeks, won't be long now. He'll sleep in your crib, maybe even wear your old clothes.'

'Are you going to give me away?' I said.

They laughed together. 'Oh, Salt, we'll keep you for ever,' my mother said. The water lapped my hands and legs and splashed into my mouth.

'That's our Salt,' my father said, rubbing my head.

Salt was the name I gave myself. I had another name, but that one didn't count.

September came, and soon my mother's belly grew big enough for two or three bellies. We stopped going out to the lake and spent more time inside the house because the first cold air of the season had already moved down the mountainside and through the streets of Salt Lake City and then out west to where we lived. On some evenings I sat at my window and watched the city in the distance. One morning my father brought me into the living room to where my mother lay on the couch and slotted one of his films into the player and shut the blinds and lit a fire to take the chill out of the air.

My mother said something strange then. She reached out and touched my hand and said, 'You are such a sensitive little boy. I wish you would speak more. Can you do that for me? Anything you want to say.'

I did not know what to say, so I said nothing.

My father opened a big book and asked me to sit beside him on the couch. I did and saw that the book had pictures in it. One of them was a large thumb bent inside a circle. He put his finger on it.

'That's where your brother is,' he said. The television screen floated in my mother's eyes as he placed the open page beside her belly.

'You brother is here,' he said.

Although he didn't explain it, I realized then that the pink thumb was my brother and the circle was what he lived in inside my mother.

'What does he breathe?' I said.

My mother looked at my father and smiled. 'Your brother, well he's breathing water,' she said.

'That's hard,' I said, 'breathing water.'

'Only for a while,' my father said, 'and when he's born he'll breathe air, just like you did.'

'Can we go to the lake now?' I said.

They looked at each other and my father went to the window and opened the blinds with the side of his hand.

'Looks fine out. What do you want to do, Mary?'

'Yes, why not – let's go,' she said. My father put biscuits and tea and blankets in the car and we drove to the edge of the lake. The morning sun put its finger into the water and stirred some pale blue paint around and around. As my father spread the blankets I knelt into the water and put my head underneath and opened my eyes, but the water stung and I came up fast. But I'd felt something in the water, maybe ten yards away, something in the current.

I lay back so that my eyes and nose were above the surface and the rest of me floated underneath.

I heard words come through the water. I sat up.

'Salt, I said you'll get a cold,' my father said. He was lying down too, on the shoreline in my mother's arms, and inside her there was a little lake where my brother was floating. So there were four of us all lying down.

A week came when my mother stayed home all the time. My father called the house every hour, and every hour she picked up the phone and said, 'Not yet.' And sometimes she said after listening for a while, 'I'm fine, Paul. Don't worry.'

But she looked worried, and the lines on her face moved across her forehead like ripples in the lake when the wind blew, which happened more now that the days were shorter and colder.

I tugged at her blouse. She replaced the phone.

'Yes, Salt?'

'What's my brother's name?'

She wiped her forehead and walked to the couch, taking lots of breaths and small steps. My brother and his little lake must have been heavy. I followed her. After she sat down, she said,

'What would you like his name to be?'

'But I don't know what he looks like yet,' I said. 'If I gave him a name and he looks different, it could be the wrong name.'

My mother stared at me a moment and her face wrinkled into a laugh. When my father called again, she told him what I had said, listened to the phone a minute and then said to me, 'Your father thinks that's a good idea – we should wait until we know what your brother looks like before we give him a name.'

That evening when he came back from work, my father brought home a jungle and carried it into the house in four or five trips: a wood chair, a wood table, a small wood

pen, and an entire wood floor which he spent the following evening hammering down. His job was cutting up
wood in a lumber yard, and all day he bent and sawed it to
size for customers. Sometimes he called where he worked
'the lumbar yard' and pointed to his lower back. Whatever
the case, now my brother's room was a forest of new furniture. This baby was important, I could tell, and while my
room was not as nice, I did not mind at all, and while my
father made the new floor, my mother sat with me watching television. Because she worked in an office where they
made advertisements, often she pointed to the screen – 'I
made that – and that.'

Now she put my hand to her stomach. The windows
were open although it was night, and even though my
hand remained there for a minute, the baby did not move
inside. I thought that maybe he was listening to my heart
through my fingertips, maybe his ear was pressed to her
skin from underneath, his eyes closed, and he was learning
about me through my heartbeats – and there was even
more: when I took my hand away my mother murmured,
and I knew he had moved. Since my parents were waiting
for the baby to be born, I realized that the baby was the one
deciding when to come out of my mother's belly, and if he
was too comfortable swimming in all that water, which
must have been warm, and not hitting anything and never
getting lost, he might want to stay there – yes, what if he
didn't want to come out, what then? I decided to ask this
question at another time because my father was hammering
away at the new floor and my mother was watching television.

And what must it be like not to have a name? When the

baby thought about himself, he didn't think of a name. So I thought of one for him. I kept it to myself.

It would also be hard for him to imagine life on the outside and I wondered how I could explain what air was and how to breathe it. He needed to know this. I was already worried. What if the doctors and my parents forgot to tell him what to do? I went to my room and got some pages and wrote in crayon on top of a sheet of paper: 'AIR', and then below it, 'You pull the air in like a rope through your nose and down into your belly, then you push out the rope. You do this thousands of times a day. If you try to count, you will forget. If you stop, you will be dead, so you have to keep doing it if you want to be alive.'

But in case my brother thought breathing thousands of times a day too hard, I decided to tell him that he would-n't have to remember anything, that it would go on even when he was asleep, and that when he ran around and played he would breathe faster, a lot more air, but it didn't matter if millions of other people breathed too, there was enough for everyone.

He must have been able to see through at least a little of the water, so I wrote, 'You see when there are things and they are in your eyes. If you move your head or they go behind you, you do not see them. But they are still there, even if you don't see them.'

I wrote all of this carefully and in big writing on three pages and brought them to where my mother slept. Without waking her, I placed the first one flat on her belly so the baby could read it, and I shone a light on to the paper so the words stood out and he could read easier. When I put the second page on her belly, the baby moved, so I knew he was reading. My mother woke up and frowned.

I said, 'I'm showing him how I breathe.'

She looked at the light and the pages. And she nodded. Her eyes filled up with water from her belly.

I presumed I would have to give up my seat at the table and in the car and that my mother might not even notice me any more or even hug me. If she didn't I would understand. My brother, no matter what his name, was new and I wasn't. I was old now. They would take him to the lake and lie with him and play with him all day. But I was happy for him.

A Saturday and Sunday went by and still no baby. My father stayed at home on Monday waiting for my brother, but no baby that day either. My mother told him to go to work the next day.

'Are you sure?' he said.

'Yes, I'll be fine. One of us has to work,' she said.

All that week and the next weekend, no baby. But on the Monday, my mother stumbled to the phone and said,

'It's time. Now. Now!'

She staggered to the couch and lay down. I ran back and forward, bringing nothing to nowhere. An ambulance was coming, she said, not to worry. The ambulance must have been lost for a while because it was thirty minutes coming and by the time it came my mother was groaning, and my dad got back at the same time, complaining about two ambulances and different companies. My brother must have been bursting to get out if he was causing all that trouble. There must have been something in there with him that made him so uncomfortable all of a sudden: nothing for nine months, and now all he wanted to do was to get out of my mother as fast as he could.

Before my father followed the ambulance to the hospital he brought me to stay with one of the neighbours, Mr Swan, who used to work but then got old and now stayed in his house all day watching television. Only then did my father race off, his long legs in his black shoes running after the ambulance that was carrying my mother who was carrying my brother.

Mr Swan's house was very quiet. He turned to me. 'Would you like a biscuit? I have biscuits.'

That evening Mr Swan heard a car drive by and walked to the window and said, 'They're back, you can go meet your new brother', and I ran out of the house and down a few doors and up the driveway and into the open door of the hallway but could not see my parents, so I searched the bags on the floor for the baby. No baby in the first bag. Searched the others. No baby. The house was silent. My father came out of their bedroom and lifted me up and squeezed me.

'Can I meet my new brother? Can I?' I said.

He shook his head. 'No, Salt, he stayed in the hospital with your mother.'

'How long for?' I said. 'I want to see my brother.'

'She'll be in the hospital till tomorrow,' he said.

I went to the fridge calendar and erased the big green crayon circle and moved it one box to the right and waited until the next day. So tomorrow my mother brings my brother home.

Tomorrow took all day to come, and when it finally did,

my father made no attempt to go to the hospital to get the baby. My mother arrived mid-morning in a taxi with a nurse and went straight to my father in their bedroom, but no baby. The nurse left and they stayed in the room with the door closed. I sat on my bed and kept the door open a little. At noon my father went into the living room and shortly afterwards I heard a film play on the television. Twenty minutes. No one made a move. If I went out to play now, they might forget to go to pick him up, so I sat on the bed and watched through the space in the door until my father walked into the kitchen and went into my mother's bedroom. I heard low talking, heard her sobbing. He came out and his hand pushed open my door.

'There you are.' He smiled. 'We were wondering.'

But his eyes were not smiling, and after a moment I began to cry too.

SALT 2

After my new brother died, my mother had to go back to the hospital for more rest, a different rest than she got at home, my father said. I had to stay with Mr Swan while my father was at work and listen to the silence as Mr Swan sat by the window until he switched on the television or got to saying something, which wasn't often.

When my mother came back from the hospital she looked a little too rested. She was very quiet and moved slower, spoke softer. Maybe she had got a bit of the disease that killed my brother. She brought back a bag with her that had two bottles of pills in it and placed these carefully side by side in the cabinet above the kitchen countertop. Every morning after that I saw her open the cabinet and open the pillboxes, take one tablet from each and swallow them with water. Those were the pills that kept her quiet and took away the shaking and the crying. Well, they may have done that, but they took some of my mother with the crying. My father became quiet too, like an empty bathtub. The clothes were put away. Someone who was supposed to have lived did not. That much I understood. My mother then seemed to love me more. Hold me tighter. Maybe the baby had been born inside me instead.

When she did say something, it came from nowhere, and you had to be ready. A few days later my parents were sitting watching a film and I was walking into the room when she said,

'Paul, look', and pointed to a baby's sweater. She looked very upset. My father grabbed it.

'I'm so sorry, Mary. I was putting some things together to donate.'

'He would have been crawling in a few months.'

'Mary, stop,' my father said. 'You can't do this to yourself. Mary, he's dead. He's gone.'

I was standing by the door. They did not see me or hear me because I was so like a ghost that I could not have been seen. Then I thought that maybe I did not exist at all. Maybe I was not born either. Or maybe my father was talking about me, not the baby.

Either way, my mother cried for the rest of the evening.

Later, when she went to bed, I came in and sat beside him. Because he was quieter now too, we did not say anything for a while until I turned to him and said,

'Did my brother count?'

'Did he count what?' he said.

'Did he live? Was he counted?'

My father put his head down. When he looked up he said, 'He lived. He was alive. At night we heard him kicking and moving and even laughing once.'

So I decided that my bother was born after all but had been taken away somewhere, a secret place. But why? Was he special? And the toys and the crib – I found them under the stairs. Why did my parents keep them if my brother was gone? Unless he was coming back.

And my father said, 'He was your brother. You had a brother, Salt.'

The sweater that made my mother cry taught me that things were not just things, they had places and times attached to them, or things that might have been, and even if they never existed, somehow they did. I would have to be careful to know the difference.

The next morning, after he left for work but before my mother got up, I stood on a chair and hitched myself up to the kitchen counter and opened the cabinet doors. There they were, the pills that stole my mother. I read the labels, pronouncing each letter, first A–L–P–R–A–Z–O–L–A–M, before repeating the word out loud:

'Alphie's Pram,' I said. 'Take two daily or as needed. Two refills.'

The other pillbox, which she hadn't opened, had the letters L–O–R–A–Z–E–P–A–M, which I then said aloud: 'Lori's Pram. Take one daily as needed. Two refills.'

When I finished reading I held out the pillboxes, one in each hand at arm's length, and spoke to them both:

'It says my mother can take you twice a day as needed. It doesn't say you can take my mother.'

She took two weeks off work. When the pills ran out she went back to the bag she brought home from Pharmalak and started in on those. Then she went back to the doctor and got two more refills. I saw it on the labels when I checked. My mother now spoke so little that I sometimes had to speak for her. When she sat on the couch in front of the television, I saw the light open and close like a fist in her eyes. It used to be once that she would ask me about my room and why it wasn't clean. Now I had to do the whole conversation myself:

'Hello, mother,' I said and stepped to the side.

'Salt, did you make up your room?' I said to myself.

A step back again. 'No, not yet. I wanted to but—'

A step to the right. 'No buts. Do it now.'

I did not step aside to answer but walked to my room and opened the door wide and began to clean. My mother lay on her bed. I saw part of her head on the pillow from the hall. I hoped she would notice, but I heard her speak into a phone instead.

'Yes, Monday I go back to work. Yes, feeling a little better, but you know it's – yes, I know. I will. Bye.'

She went to work that Monday, but it made no difference because she did not get her easy voice back, her easy steps. I lived with half my mother from that time on.

Once I asked her where my brother was. I tried to make it sound like a normal question. 'If he stayed in the hospital,' I said, 'was he buried there?'

She shook her head. 'The angels took your brother, Salt.'

At last I had an answer. So the angels took him. Never gave him a chance. They could have done something, they could have asked God. I had it in for angels after that, because that's what my mother said: she said – and I heard her say this very, very clearly – she said, 'The angels took your brother.'

I played by the lake on my own from then on, even during the spring and summer months. One evening I stayed late, until the sun went down, and I wanted to go home because I knew my parents would be worried, but the house was close by and I was almost six years old now, and I felt strange anyway. I was careful, though, because I didn't want any angels to snatch me.

That was the night I saw a boy come out of the water.

I didn't actually see him but he was there. He told me a lot of things that made sense. He told me that the world was made up, that the angels were thieves all right. Don't believe anything anyone tells you. He said that I was never a baby myself and that my parents were made up. Angels, they were nasty things. This made sense because why else would they have stood by and let my brother not be born? The world was made up. The people in it were made up. When I turned my back they disappeared.

I stuck my head below the water to see him, but all I heard was the sloshing, the roar in my ears. I squinted in the dark fighting the pain of the salt in my eyes, all black, nothing but the black water, the pale white bed, maybe some cold currents brushing my arms, a presence somewhere off to the front, but nobody, nothing; so I didn't actually see the boy. I stayed underneath until I had to come up for air. And when the cold air pressed my face I knew that I had made him up too.

Silence grew like a plant along the walls and the windows of our house. Because my brother was not born alive, he stayed instead in our thoughts, like the electricity that runs in wires along the floorboards and turns on all the lamps but is never seen. That's how my brother lived in us, in me, and why I remembered him always.

SALT 3

Twelve years passed like a bandage.

One day my father came home from work with a strange cough, and in a couple of weeks it had grown in him like a vine that ran little wires through his lungs and also through the house, through the walls; I lay at night in bed and listened to him struggle. Then he got a stomach ache that made dull spoons of his eyes, and barely a week later he looked as if ten years had been added to his forty-five.

He continued to work in the lumber yard attached to a large home improvement store where he prepared special orders and cut the wood to size, and if no special orders came, he stacked the incoming wood using his forklift. But most of the time he was the man who cut the wood, and I think I knew why he liked that job. He wore his earmuffs, his goggles, his apron and special gloves, and he operated the large precision saw in his own space, a fenced-off part of the store by the yard, away from customers and away from the rest of the world. I wondered what he thought about to fill the time every day since he was so good at his job. On evenings and weekends I often found him in his armchair in the living room watching black-and-white movies taken from four shelves of video tapes, maybe three hundred films, most taped off the television and titled with a black felt-tip pen on the labels. I stood at the door behind him and saw the flashing lights from the television and saw his face in the dark, often smiling in a kind of peace, because he was a lonely man, even if that's where his happiness lay, smiling as if the film were a ship he'd lost contact with and found again.

But he contacted something else, too, that made his skin pale and the spoons harden. He went to the doctor who put a scope to his chest and made him breathe deeply, tapped him here and there like a wall before the nail is hammered in. That doctor then referred him to another doctor, and my father made the appointment straight away because my father had a job and health insurance; the second doctor had him tested and scanned. The results came back in a couple of days. When the doctor called and asked my father to come to his office to pick up the results, I knew that the vine must have shown up somewhere on the map, and I guessed it was that same vine of silence that started growing after my brother died. Anyway, my father brought home a lot of pills from the doctor's office and lined them up on the kitchen counter, taking one of them every day. He did not get better. I often held the pillboxes in my hands and urged them on. They looked like better pills to me because he was still the same father to me, still a happy man after taking them, unlike what happened to my mother with those pram pills.

The second doctor referred him to a specialist, who suggested an operation to remove portions of his stomach and lungs, but my father said that he would first like to give the medication more time to do its work. At home, he joked about the pills, shaking them like salt at the dinner table, putting the several pillboxes sidewards along the floor in a golf stroke using his umbrella.

'Soon I'll be the Pillsbury Boy,' he said to me, smiling and patting his stomach. I knew then that we would lose him. After two months, he began taking days off, so the store hired a part-timer to fill in for him. I could see how much it hurt my dad to lose his space in the yard; still he had other things on his mind: when he was alone with my mother I heard him talk about health insurance, heard it from my room, heard him tell her how he couldn't afford to lose it. The words drifted starkly into my room, separate from the bodies that spoke them, as if they were looking for an audience, they were that important.

'I have to keep this job. Remember what happened to Bernard Simmons and his wife? They lost their insurance and look at what happened to them when their child got sick.'

'Didn't they lose their house?' my mother said.

'The child was two months in the hospital with a brain tumour. Thank God everything went well, but first the car went—'

'They sold it and borrowed his brother's second car.'

'Then they had this yard sale and she had all her silver out there on the lawn.'

'I bought it,' my mother said, 'and gave it back to her.'

'You did?'

'I knew you wouldn't mind. She was so happy to see it again. I think it was her mother's.'

'And then the older son had to drop out of college when the child had a relapse. You could tell they were arguing and not sleeping. Then one day—'

'They were gone,' my mother said. 'A For Sale sign on the lawn. Packed their bags and left in the middle of the night. I heard her crying, got up and went outside, but they were already down the street.'

'I heard they moved back to his grandparents with their children. Must be tough on everyone. The grandparents had their own life going on, and now suddenly it's a full house again.'

I lay in bed and felt the words hover over me. I did remember the Simmons five doors down, how their lives changed over three or four months. When the child first goes into hospital everyone supports them, then the insurance company says that the money has run out, they've reached their limit. So out come the posters in the local stores, 'Support Andy Simmons's Brain Tumour Operation'. Picture of little smiling Andy sitting on a blanket on the floor. The jar beside the picture filled with loose change from the groceries. Weeks pass and less and less money drops into the jar. People stop noticing the receptacle at the cash register; it joins the other jars in their mind, the ones for car washes at the school, renovations to the church, the girl scouts. Emily Partridge, a neighbour's daughter, was caught with her hand 'delaying' in the jar, and the cashier said it was unclear whether she was putting some money in or taking some out. Maybe both.

A season passed and Andy passed from people's minds, cropping up in the odd yard sale and an occasional article in the papers with the same photo of Andy on the blanket. News was that the tumour shrank, but so too did the lives of the Simmons family. I called over often, every time noticing less and less furniture in the house: a couple of chairs missing, then that big ornate mirror they kept over the fireplace, a general bareness filling the place, and how she wrung her hands and smiled when I called because fewer people stopped to visit them now and they were invited to fewer parties, fewer trips. Some things were added to their lives, such as the oil stain on the driveway where he'd changed the car oil himself instead of bringing it to the garage, the clothes they wore for longer, and how they stayed home more. And all the while in that hospital the child lay on his bed. I wondered if in the back of their minds they saw him as having taken everything from them, their belongings, their friends, their savings. Maybe they thanked him for taking friends like that. In the end, though, they drove down an empty street in the middle of the night and away from their lives because their child got sick and they lost the insurance. And where the insurance went, their lives soon followed.

After three months my father had missed so many days at work that he was fired. I found the letter from his employer in the letterbox, the one that terminated his position, and I handed it to him while he watched a movie, a scene where Humphrey Bogart was steering a small boat down a river, and my father opened the envelope that shone in the light of the screen. I saw him read the letter. Then he folded it and put into his breast pocket, turned to me and smiled.

Some days later he answered an advertisement he saw on the back page of the local paper. His unsteady index finger prodded the numbers out of the telephone on the table by his armchair and he announced his name into the handset but accidentally hung up and then had to dial again and once more say his name. He listened and then spoke again.

'I'm calling about the advertisement in the *Salt Lake City Tribune* for research volunteers for an experimental medicine.' I heard him give his details, talk about an interview. 'Yes. Three o'clock. In the Pharmalak building. With Dr Fargoon – I'm sorry, Mr Fargoon. Yes, yes, I'll be there. Tomorrow.'

My mother floated in and out of the living room. I knew she couldn't wait to hear what he told her. Her eyes were red as if she used them for more than seeing, as if she had stuffed every bad thing in the world into them and tried to see anyway, and that can't be done. I was young and I knew that much, but she was a woman full to the top with compassion, and that was something I did not know then, not the way I do now.

He held out his arms and she bent into them, and he said, 'They say I can go up there to their facility in Park City. Tomorrow. No guarantees, but I may get on a trial medication.' And she sobbed for joy, like every tear was a small hand grabbing at hope. I moved away from the door, relieved that there was happiness in the house, that the air felt so much lighter and easier to breathe.

That evening, while we were all on the couch watching *Lawrence of Arabia*, he asked me to drive the next day. It should have been obvious, I thought, because my mother didn't drive and he wasn't going to have a ghost's chance of even getting out the driveway, and it occurred to me that being sick meant you relied completely on others and you took nothing for granted: one step, then the next step.

During the intermission part of the film, my mother and I spread a map under the kitchen light and studied it even though we'd been to Park City a few times, or driven through it on the way to Missoula, Montana, where we stayed in a mountain cabin some summers before. Park City was a high mountain resort, founded by Irish miners before being turned into a ski resort, and now the home of a pharmaceutical company and private hospital, Pharmalak.

The next morning my dad banged on my bedroom wall with the broomstick, three thuds, and a 'Are you up yet, Salt?'

It used to be a job getting me out of bed. I remembered my mother often calling, then shouting, then yelling at me to 'get up and go to school'. They were the three stages of my alarm clock, and I usually didn't stir until the yelling started, that being the final stage. My dad discovered a few years before that the broomstick on the bedroom wall was far more effective and that I always jumped out of bed, though he used it sparingly. If the broomstick thudded on the wall I knew it was important, whereas my mother's calls for school seemed more mechanical, something she did while she made coffee and toasted the bread: 'Get up, get up, get up.'

And so the broomstick tapped the wall, and indeed I did jump out of bed, shouting, 'Yes, I'm up, I'm up!'

After breakfast my mother and I helped my father out to the car and eased him in; when he was comfortable she put the picnic blanket over him, and for a moment I thought how better it would be to go to the lake instead and spend the day there.

It was a forty-minute drive to Park City. We pulled up to the glass doors and helped him out. He waited on a bench while I parked, and then we all walked in together across the lobby and into a café, where a woman in a white coat and with a clipboard came out to join us. I wondered where this Fargoon fellow was.

'Hi, I'm Jane,' she said, and turned to my father, 'and you must be Paul.'

She was too businesslike, I didn't like the way she called him by his first name as if he were an invalid, a nursing-home resident, someone whose brain lived in another place and time, playing with people long dead, who might respond to a first name better than a surname.

'And I have some questions for you, Paul. If you can read these forms and answer the questions, that would be great,' she said.

My father nodded and examined the forms eagerly, going over them with my mother as Jane watched him and I watched Jane. I could tell she was evaluating him, and that the interview was happening now, that she was making up her mind now based on how he acted and wrote. The answers to the questions were most likely a formality. When he handed the forms back I knew it was all for nothing because she smiled even wider, the type of smile you get when you are about to hear the word 'No.'

'Now I have these, and that's great,' she said. 'I'm going to discuss these responses with Mr Fargoon and the drug trial coordinator, Dr Miller.'

She stood. 'Can I get you anything at the café?'

'No, thanks,' my father said. He had the soft eyes of a man in hope. I couldn't watch.

'Then I'll be back in about fifteen minutes,' she said and left, not before saying, 'It was very nice to meet you.' Some people smile like a knife.

My father unfurled the newspaper we brought in the car, always a man for the world news, and my mother got up to get coffee. I wandered the café and crossed the lobby and into a hallway and found an open door into an exhibition room; I passed a sign with The Hall of Cylinders written in amber.

The room smelled of wood polish and swam in a warm colour between yellow and orange. I saw five glass cylinders lined on each side, spaced out over twenty feet, each cylinder about ten feet high by six wide, with marble inlays on the floor around each. In the middle of the room a fountain dribbled over some rocks. I moved to the right and read the description of the cylinders on that side, 'The Sick Man Exhibit', and continued on by 'Tuberculosis Man', 'Influenza Man', 'Alzheimer's Man', 'Cancer Man' and 'Mental Disease Man', all with their own scenery and figures; it was like walking along a column of Greek statues.

In the first one a wax figure of a man lay on a bed in a dormitory with both arms resting straight on blue and white sheets. Behind the man a window opened on to a green lawn, and the curtains were rendered in motion, as if a breeze blew into the tube itself, and someone had etched a description of the disease on the glass at the back of the tube.

Scientists have found decay from *mycobacterium tuberculosis* in the spinal column of Egyptian mummies. The disease that killed them – children, women, men, slaves, kings – remains entombed with its victims after four thousand years.

I circled the tube for the rest of the passage around to the sick man's right side and imagined I was visiting him. At any second, the man might glance up and ask me how his chart looked, or worse, ask who I was, and if I could please let him go. I decided to ignore tuberculosis man if he said anything, especially something like 'I'm better now and I want to go home.' Walking a wax man home was not going to happen to me today.

To read further I had to go all the way behind tuberculosis man, so that if anyone walked in and looked, I appeared to be standing inside the tube myself.

Tuberculosis was killed with fresh air and drugs. By the 1950s, patients filled over one hundred thousand beds in sanatoriums throughout the United States. On November 20, 1940, the antibiotic streptomycin was given to the first man.

I walked to the front of the tube again and watched the man lying there, how he looked at peace. When I heard my own breathing, I felt the silence in the hall grow on me and moved on to the second cylinder on the right side, 'Influenza Man'. It showed men in sports gear standing around a track gripping batons. I pressed a button on the tube that said 'play', and the runners instantly dashed from the starting line toward a sickly figure a hundred metres ahead of them, limping around the first bend in the track.

Since the beginning of the Christian calendar, approximately forty people have lived – that is, forty generations measured in the life of one person in that generation. Therefore we differ little from our historical ancestors, since human evolution takes place over thousands of years, not hundreds.

The runners made up half the distance in seconds. Their faces were blank and they all wore the same black outfits and black shoes. The portly figure ahead of them sported a large flapping yellow shirt and glanced back in terror as they gained on him.

A parasite organism can go through 2,000 generations in a month, about 180,000 years in human life, so viruses live and die at a rate that lets us see them evolve. When a virus strikes it is usually in two waves, the first to learn our response, the second as its major assault, and that's when disaster strikes. In 1918, a flu virus killed twenty million people.

They were upon the sick man at the one hundred metres mark. The man dropped and sprawled on the track as the runners in black powered round the next bend and handed over their batons. I wished we could forget people like viruses do and at once looked behind me, as if I had been touched with a baton, and tried to see my parents in the café: I had been thinking of my father and how I would miss him, how it might be easier to forget him by pressing a button, and if I could do it.

I moved to the third cylinder, 'Alzheimer's Man', where a woman sat in an armchair on a front porch with a blanket over her lap. She stared but not at anything in particular, as if her gaze had no direction or had not found what it wanted to see, or did not discern what it needed to see, while several sad-looking people stood around her. I pressed the play button.

The young girl depicted at the woman's side moved and said, 'Mother, can you hear me? Do you remember me?'

I went straight to the fifth cylinder, 'Mental Disease Man'. Inside, three figures, a woman, a man, and a child, stood with drooped heads as if suspended from a string. Behind them, stark black text overlaid an ice-green background.

The first asylums appeared in the fifteenth century, sometimes doubling as institutions that cared for lepers. In 1547 Henry VIII donated the buildings of the Priory of St Mary of Bethlehem to the city as a mental hospital. In time it became known as 'Bedlam' and was a favourite day trip for city people who bought tickets to observe the bedlam inside – the screaming, the convulsions, the fighting – until well into the nineteenth century.

I backed away to the cylinders on the other side. The first housed a tablet set on a velvet-lined silver case with a chemical name inscribed underneath, and above the pill, straight lines and spheres illustrated its chemical structure. Someone had carefully inscribed the word 'Streptomycin' beneath the model of the pill. Under that, in smaller writing, 'The first antibiotic to combat tuberculosis. 1940'.

The pill hall of fame.

The next cylinder contained penicillin, the third a

painkiller, the fourth a beta blocker. I did not see a pill in the fifth cylinder opposite 'Mental Disease Man' – the great cure to come for mental disease.

I looked back at the wheelchair woman who happened to be staring straight at me. So that's what she was looking at, searching for the anxiety pill that isn't born yet. Maybe she was in the wrong cylinder. These things happen. Maybe she heard and understood everything her family said to her and didn't like them enough to say anything back. Maybe she was just anxious and didn't know what to say. Or maybe her brain had forgotten the list of things to do in her body every day and was looking for that list but didn't know where it left the piece of paper, and in its place, the mind sat like an empty orchard where all the apples were stolen but the trees were still standing and the autumn was still in the air and the walls still surrounded the orchard – and everything was still. I renamed her 'orchard woman', an orchard with no apples.

You could do worse than live in a cylinder with your history written behind you, your accomplishments, your defeats, the names of those who grew up with you, and opposite you in another cylinder, the one thing that defined you, your life's accomplishment, displayed in a velvet–lined silver case with drawings and explanations, your significance. You live to be a certain age, then you go to the hall of cylinders where people come to visit you every now and then, read some writing, feel the peace of the place, standing out of time, out of the city.

But they already had such places. They were called graveyards.

When I looked back at the empty cylinder, the lights flickered and I saw the shadows form and reform, and in a split second I saw my father standing in the 'Cancer Man' cylinder. Half his body was missing. Pieces of his arm, his face.

I backed out and turned and looked down at the floor and followed it almost running until I came to the café and his newspaper and his fingers curled around the pages, and he looked over it and smiled at me: 'There you are, Salt. I was wondering.'

I said, 'I'm going to get a piece of bread, something to eat, do you want anything?'

'No, no, thanks.'

I was at the counter when I saw Jane return. They talked, my father nodding, Jane nodding, and I saw her place both her hands on his one hand on the table, then saw my mother's head go down. *Well*, I thought, *that's that*. But then Jane placed forms in front of him, and next thing my father was signing them.

So he had been taken for the trials. I couldn't believe it. Then my mother went upstairs with Jane. I walked over to him.

'What's going on, Dad?'

'Your mother is seeing Mr Fargoon — won't be long — he's opened a slot for her today, a consultation.'

'But he's a psychiatrist.'

My father placed a couple of sheets on the table along-side the ones he had signed, which were waivers and consents, as far as I could see.

'Now, Salt, I want you to fill these out, and I mean every space.' He handed me a pen with a still hand, and I took it and held it over the pages: an application for medical trials at Pharmalak.

He leaned forward. 'Promise me, son, that if you get a call from these people, you'll take it, you'll go. It'll be after I'm gone. Free medicine, Salt, to help you get past things, you know.'

I knew he was looking straight at me, but I couldn't look back.

'Promise me.'

'Yes.'

'And promise me you'll never leave your mother alone.'

The people sitting at the next table were watching now, one with a cup halfway to her mouth. I was embarrassed, but my father stared at me as if we were the only people in the room.

'Yes,' I said, 'I promise. I won't leave her alone.' And I signed the forms. He shuffled them straight.

After half an hour my mother and Jane came back to the table, and my father handed Jane the forms. My mother held a bag she didn't have going up. Jane said to me, probably because she felt she had to,

'Your father did not meet the criteria for the trial, but he has kindly made arrangements with us to donate his body, a gift I hope,' and she turned to him, 'that we will not receive for a very long time yet.'

The three of us sat at the table after Jane shook his hand and left. I thought of a hundred intelligent and courageous things to say but none got past my lips.

'I'm sorry Dad,' I said.

Above us, a television broadcast something about people forgetting things and what they could take for it.

We drove down the mountain. It was high summer, the

middle of July, and my father asked me to open the windows and turn on the air conditioning at the same time, and the wind blew the cool blue sky around the inside of the car. We were nearing Kimball Junction when he asked me to pull over. I helped him to the edge of a meadow as my mother spread a blanket and we relaxed in the morning air and listened to the birds sing. My father lay on his side and closed his eyes and let the sun stretch warm on his skin. My mother lay beside him and hugged him until he smiled. Then we had some sandwiches.

I lay on my back and watched a cloud find a tree in the centre of the meadow. We had come to the mountain to save him, and we left with him signing over his body to them. I thought of the cancer cylinder and imagined placing him in it and throwing it into the water so that he could remain preserved for ever, floating around the seas of the world.

Around six o'clock we packed up and drove on.

My father looked at the passing fields, the meadows, the flowers that groped at the roadside, looked at them for the last time.

He signed on to a different type of health insurance, one that cost more each month because he was paying the entire cost himself, and our family's savings dwindled. He told me he was thinking that maybe an operation was the best thing to do after all, but he had delayed too long, hoping the pills would work, and when he lost that more expensive insurance after four or five months he visited the specialist less because he could not afford the bills; the specialist, though understanding, said he had a business to run.

A month after that, my father couldn't afford any doctors at all any more. I wished he were more assertive, would get in people's faces, shout a little. Sometimes I passed my parents' bedroom and saw him sitting in a chair by the bed, his head in his hands, and glimpsed the grey terror on him.

He decided to get the operation done after all, but it was then explained to him that he now had no health insurance coverage and that, therefore, the operation would have to remain on hold. The specialist said that perhaps he might feel well enough to get a job and then proceed with the operation, since everything was ready and the operation would probably cure his condition. There was every reason, the specialist said, to feel confident. Therefore, all my father needed was some coverage or the money to pay for the procedure, the specialist said.

Using the rest of the family's savings, my father enrolled in a health plan where there were no doctors – at least the type you went to see – and where the drugs arrived in the mail. But because he wasn't working and on a health plan, the medicine cost a lot more money and the savings ran out altogether. Soon enough I heard the same disembodied words float from their room into mine.

'Can we write a cheque for this month's premium?' she said.

'Yes, yes. I'm selling some of the collector films I have. I got a good price. That will pay for this month.'

He offered to sell all his videos but nobody wanted them, just the rare stuff. We had our own yard sale then, but there was no jar in the supermarket because grown men don't get jars. That's for children. And when the money ran out, the pills stopped coming in the mail, which is when the pain grew, layers of long pain, pain lined up around the corner and all the way to the end of the street, pain that talked to itself while it waited to get into his body; and eventually, ten months after he had first come home with the vine growing in him, my father's body formed entirely into wires.

I held his hand every evening before bedtime. It felt like underbrush on a forest floor. I wanted to rip the vine out of him, but if I had, nothing of him would have remained. I could have gathered him up and carried him as he did me when I was a child, but I would have been carrying sticks. When he did not stop moaning, we rushed him to hospital, where one morning, close to noon, he died.

I did not remember the men who came to the hospital mortuary to put my father into a funeral hearse, or my mother and I walking behind it for a few hundred years, or was it yards, both dressed in black, until we got to the mortuary chapel, where I stood outside a holding room as my mother sat with him and cried, even though she kept it as quiet as she could. I did not remember entering that room and standing there, looking into that box, he and I the only ones there, apart from the utter, complete silence. His eyes were closed and his skin white as china. I did not remember spending a minute waiting to touch him, and how his forehead was a stone under my kiss. I did not remember walking away. I did not remember the hearse turning away from the hospital, turning for the mountains, his body in that coffin, not going down into the earth but up into the mountains to where he had promised it. And my mother and I walked around the neighbourhood for an hour and said nothing, and then we went home. I did not remember, because to remember you first have to forget.

His old work friends arrived and one of them handed my mother his goggles and apron; she made sandwiches and served coffee to those who came, then after the people went home she went to bed and cried; I stayed up watching television until the sun rose, and then I went for a walk. That was the day.

Beginning the next morning I went for walks every few hours, crossing neighbourhoods and finding new streets, and when I got back to the house again I expected to see him in his armchair reading a newspaper or watching the ghosts on the screen. That's the thing about dead people. Your brain won't let them go and keeps on the lookout for them. Dead person coming down the stairs, dead person waking you up, dead person bringing you to school, dead person watching television. Dead person. My dad.

SALT 4

My mother and I managed to remain in our small house near the lake shore, though she hardly worked at all now and the letterbox filled with bills and the bank started to call and leave messages saying they must insist that sums be paid, thirty days, sixty days late, form messages with her name filled in. But every morning the light brought white salt and blue sky to my bedroom window, and after the sun went down I heard the salt's white silence while I waited to sleep.

And the pills came too. A couple of weeks after my father died she went to the doctor's and came back with more Alprazolam and Lorazepam and another container she never opened that had some kind of stimulants to make her more lively if she needed it. I arranged them for her in the kitchen cabinet. She took one morning and night: they were the sun and moon of her day. I figured they must be good if she can take them for twelve years, so that first night, after I arranged them in the cabinet, I tried one.

No one would miss one pill.

That night I thought I saw some lights reflect off my bedroom window. It was about midnight and I could not sleep. I sat up in bed, went to the window and looked outside, because although it was freezing I had left it open for the fresh air. After I parted the blinds completely, the moon came into view, siphoning cool light on to the desert mountains and the dirty white salt crystals that stretched for miles over the dry bed of the Great Salt Lake. Once as wide as Utah, the lake had receded to an empty, flat surface that existed only as silence − that is, until the night I saw those lights.

I turned my face right, toward the city, about ten miles away, and then ahead to the shallow water of the lake and Antelope Island. Nothing moved. I waited, sure that I had seen something until − yes, there they were again − they beamed now, pinpricks of light coming from my left, from the white desert that stretched to the Nevada border an hour's drive away, split by a single road. I wondered what anyone was doing out there, especially at night.

I turned on my bed, or was it the window? I was unsure if I was asleep or awake or somewhere in the middle. My thoughts seemed off to the side. Come back thoughts. I liked the feeling because there was no feeling. I watched as an engine droned across the salt, that's what it sounded like, and then more small lights flickered and bounced out from the dark all together as if they had been waiting for the engine. They were joined by other lights, and so many arrived that I thought there must have been hundreds. Now and again a light or two moved away, then returned to the group. And after half an hour the lights parted and drifted off singly into the night. Within just a few minutes, all had left, and the lake bed was empty and dark again. Then I heard more engines drone for five minutes, and then nothing. I lay back on my bed, and the breeze let me sleep, and sleep showed me pictures. Sometimes sleep was dark, sometimes there were lights, sometimes pictures.

I fell asleep – for sure, I mean.

Well, didn't they follow me in there, into my dreams, the shadows that were carrying those lights: some women, some men and some children, never close enough to have faces, but shadows that wandered across the salt. And when I walked close to them in my sleep, my heart raced and skipped and jumped because I was afraid they might see me dreaming them and approach.

But that was not the part that frightened me. I saw their faces, and among them the faces of my parents. And out from between them, mine.

The next morning, when I was getting my mother her morning dose, I slipped another pill into my mouth. I did that for a few days as each day crossed namelessly into the next. Could have been days, could have been weeks. The pills kept me pressed down and out of any place where I might feel too much. Sometimes it seemed as if my mind were held onto my brain with a thin piece of string. I waited for the lights on most nights, even if it was much colder now and I felt tired, until one night when I opened the windows wide to stay awake and the room filled with white pale light from the salt whose smell scoured its way down to my lungs. I lit a candle and put it on the window sill to warm my hands while I watched: if the lights on the salt saw me, I'd look like a spirit, a face in the long night with no body. If the lights saw me, they might say, 'There's Salt. He's lost his body!'

That's what it felt like now and then, that I had no body

and I wanted that — that was a good thing under the circumstances.

On one of those nights a door closed from inside the
house and I guessed my mother was probably in her room,
where she spent most of her time since my father's death.
She spoke less too, walking around the house like a body
anonymous to itself, and she touched fewer things, maybe
a glass for water, the handle of a closet for a cup, the lid of
the coffee maker. The house remained mostly undisturbed
around her, and most of the time I didn't know she'd been
out of her room until I heard her door close again. But
now I understood how the pills made a ghost of her, she
swallowed so many of them, and it was all for the better.
The less you feel, the less sad you are.

I left the window and walked the corridor. 'Mother, are
you okay?'

'Yes, I am.'

'Can I get you anything?'

'No, no, dear — I'll see you in the morning, okay?'

I waited a moment, my hand on the door.

'Who is out on the salt?'

'No one, dear. That was just your father, that was just a
story he liked to tell, that's all, a fairy tale.'

'But I can see—'

'I have to sleep. You know, I have to sleep. Tomorrow.'

'Tomorrow,' I said. 'Goodnight.'

Her room darkened under the door. I went back to my
own bedroom and the window. When I looked out, the
glass was full of them. The lights were there again, about a
mile away. But one light was a lot closer, a light flickering
down by the highway, less than five minutes' walk, maybe

someone who couldn't sleep out taking a stroll. I was still dressed, and no one went for walks out there, even in moonlight, so curiosity overcame me and I put on a coat and cap and boots and left the house, turned left and walked to the end of the street, turned right, crossed the highway, and jogged along the other side until I reached the salt. I stepped on to it, heard the hard crystals crunch, and looked around, waiting for a glimpse of something, of someone.

I felt the silence like a cool brick mortared across the sky and the mountains, the yellow blur of Salt Lake City to the east, and behind that the towering Wasatch mountain range. This could have been a sister country to the surface of the moon itself, that's how close it seemed. And the basin was endless on nights like this: vast, damaged, a place where you could put a foot down and step on ground untouched for a million years.

If those lights were people, heaven knows who they could be. My father had referred to them once, though it must have been just a story after all, as my mother said. Yes, he said, all the sick people ended up living on the salt, or he sometimes said when I didn't study, or if I left things lying around, that 'We'll all end up living on the salt.' 'Who's out there?' I asked, but he never told me, not even what they looked like, and when I asked my mother again, she said no one lived on the salt. They could be people marooned from the city, sick people who had given up on feeling good again, living in cars and tents, people who had fallen from the mind and then the eye of their relatives, sisters, brothers, mothers, fathers, third cousins, grandmothers, people who slipped away and never found their way back. And my father only started telling that story after he got sick. Never heard it before that.

A car approached on the road, its headlights sweeping a fan beam alongside it, and when it passed I saw a girl standing about twenty feet from me, dressed in white, and I jumped but said nothing because she was smiling and holding something out in her hands. But the car went by too fast and she went out like a match in wet fingers. I could see nothing so I ran across the salt, slipping and catching divots and small rocks, to where she stood. I reached a trail of small stone sculptures that people sometimes left on the dry bed as they drove to Nevada along the highway. Couldn't see her. I stood and listened. Nothing. When I turned to go back to the road my foot kicked over a pile of stones and a paper shunted loose. I picked it up, held it close so I could read it.

A photograph that looked like my mother when she was young and, strewn along the trail, six or seven stones pinned what looked like papers. I continued up a small hill, picked another one up, another photograph, a boy and two older people in front of a tree. Now I was higher off the salt surface, high enough to see the shallow water of the lake east of here glisten nearer the city.

'Are you there?' I said.

And nothing but the cold answered, and then the moonlight. I gripped my coat and walked back home, looking around once or twice in case she was following me, hoping she was. I undressed and got into bed, wearing my socks to keep my feet warm and my cap to keep the breeze off my head. But first I took a pill, the first time I'd taken two in any one day: two Lori's Prams, as the younger Salt might have said.

I'll take two just this once.

The next morning I woke and brought my mother some coffee because she had not left her room. I left it at her bedside and told the shape under the blankets that there was some hot coffee now, to take it if she could. And the voice from under the blankets said that she would take it in a minute. Then I sat at the kitchen table calling, 'It'll go cold.'

'I'll take it soon, Salt.'

I realized I had a problem: if I went to two tablets a day, my mother and her doctor would ask questions, since my mother always had used the same amount for the longest time never deviating from her daily dose. Yes, there was only one thing for it, I'd find the bag she got from Fargoon at Pharmalak when we visited with my father. She hadn't touched the thing since bringing it down off the mountain, maybe because it reminded her of my father's desperate trip for life.

I knew where the pills were, in the kitchen cupboard with the vacuum cleaner, still in their blue plastic bag with the PL logo on it. I crept to the cupboard and holding a flashlight I rifled a blister pack of samples and pried it open with my fingernails and in no time at all one of those Xanax was swimming its taste across my tongue before it made the dive down. Bigger pill, bigger dose, I thought, but I was used to them now, and that was okay. No point in splitting the medication. The effect was quick coming, because in less than an hour the pills had made it to my head.

That was the end of the dreams of the lights and my father's great fear of dying alone and in the wilderness, in the desert, the land of pills, what I thought his story meant. That's what I said to myself anyway, or was it someone else I said it to, or did someone else say it to me? Anyway.

I was finding it harder to concentrate, but that was a good thing under the circumstances.

I counted all the pills in the bag: two hundred and forty. That was enough for four months, but what if my mother needed some, and what if I needed to take more?

So next morning, two weeks after my father died, I called the Pharmalak number and talked to Fargoon's receptionist, the one who answered when I called the number. I told her how my father had arranged for me to participate in a drug trial, and if there were any in progress. She said she knew of my name and that, yes, they had a few clinical trials ongoing. In no time at all I was seeing the man himself on the mountain, and no end of pills were coming my way, different types and all for all the conditions I seemed to have, strange and experimental conditions, so I could mix and match at home if I wanted to, not that I did, because you have to be careful, damn careful. Some I couldn't take or didn't want to, so I did other things with the excess medicine, recreational things as well as more serious projects, even some drug trials of my own using a slingshot, but only when I had nothing better to do.

I enjoyed being a ghost. My mother and I lived better together. I bothered her less. Two ghosts now, living in the same house, at last.

Sometimes in the morning the living me broke through and asked terrible questions, but going to the closet and opening a pillbox solved that problem, and while I waited for the questions to go away, the words in my head occasionally had a life of their own because they entered and left of their own accord:

Salt around me, salt above me. Salt to my right, salt to my left. Take a good look at me now. I'm a man of salt.

SALT 5

From then on I made the trip in the train to Fargoon once a month, staying on my best behaviour for the drug trials. It was worth it, even if it meant having to tell him things about myself that were true some of the time to keep him from becoming suspicious of my motives. For five months I served my mother her pills morning and evening. She went back to work but was now a full-time ghost. She did everything living people do but she was missing all of her insides, that's all. It was a good trade for not feeling bad. I understood that now.

But another big problem surfaced, and I was surprised I hadn't stumbled across it before.

Almost five months after he died, I realized I could not find my father's body anywhere.

It was the third week of November, and I decided I'd visit him. I was sure to take my morning pills – two now – with one in my pocket for the walk to the city cemetery. The walk lasted two hours but I needed to keep moving anyway, and as soon as I entered the gates I turned to a plot where two men shovelled clay into a grave. The gravediggers knew nothing of a man buried by that name even when I said it three times in a louder voice each time and then wrote his name out for them in capital letters. The one in the red cap pulled the cigarette out of his mouth and shook his head.

'That name I don't remember. But we can check the register if you like, back at the office.' He pointed up the hill to the small brick building with a chimney with smoke coming out.

I thought about it and said, 'Thanks. I'll look for a while.'

'When did he die?' he said.

'About five months ago.'

That stopped him smoking. 'You can't find him after five months?'

'No, but I'm going to look for him today.'

He nodded and put the cigarette back in his mouth and the shovel in his hands.

I walked away from the two of them and strolled the avenues of names, even checked the new plots, and saw the crosses and monuments cover the rolling field in all directions, spreading to the skyline, bunching up against the city in the distance, with all those people lying under my feet, the green paper of grass. It was my first time here, and I never knew so many people could be dead in one place. Even though I tried to keep track of where I went, I was soon lost among the dead, and as luck would have it, no one else was visiting the cemetery that morning, no one I could ask about my father, so I ended up chancing my luck, hoping for a lucky strike. (A lucky strike means turning around and there he is, there's my dad, and I can know from then on and for the rest of my life that this is where he lies, under the rest of time.)

I looked, but I could not find my father's grave. I found

lots of fathers, but no father of mine; I read lots of dates, but no dates of birth and death that matched his. I had walked for a long time and I had questions ready, standing shoulder to shoulder, without anyone to ask them to, so I decided to go back home and mention to my mother that there was no grave: she worked downtown and would be home soon, and we could clear the whole thing up.

The two hours back to the house lasted longer because now I was carrying all the gravestones in my head, counting them and searching them again in case I'd missed something – I must have, after all. And I began to get angry at myself and at whoever hid him away like that. When I got back I changed my clothes, and though my feet hurt I went out walking again to keep myself occupied and walk away the anger, and I found a new neighbourhood, one that might yield some clues, maybe a sighting of my mother wandering lost, maybe a friendly stranger who might know what was going on; after I turned the corner into a narrow street that bordered the back yards of the houses I heard a dog yelp and stopped to listen.

The dog yelped again, longer until it fell to a whimper.

I came to a gate and saw a man raising a stick and watched the stick all the way down to a small dog, a pit bull terrier, who cowered at the end of a chain wrapped around a barrel. The dog tried to make itself smaller but the man's blow was well aimed, and the dog convulsed under it. I moved at the gate, half in and half out, and saw that the man was dull in the eyes and that his big mouth hung open, with his tongue full and moist at the lips, as if he did all his thinking with it.

The stick rose and fell, and again the dog yelped.

'What did he do?' I said.

The man paused, looked around him and spotted me, watched me a moment, said something I did not catch.

The stick rose and fell again.

'What did he do?' I said.

The man pointed the stick at me. 'I'm busy. Get lost, okay?'

The dog shrank into a ball, ears back, shivering in fear. I still had all the headstones from the graveyard in my head and it was hard to carry this too, so I turned to leave. But when the stick rose again, a hand gripped it. It can't have been my hand because I was still standing at the gate and the hand looked enormous even from where I was standing. The man glanced up because he hadn't noticed me coming for him, I moved that quickly. He tried to get my hand off the stick, but I gripped harder.

'Let go,' he said. 'I'm warning you. Get off my property.'

He kicked me in the shin and his punch caught me only in the back of my head, since I turned away just in time. Still I would not let go, and we moved across the yard, he pulling and kicking, I pulling and ducking. Then he kicked me again, this time in the knee, so I swung my elbow into his right eye. He went down, grabbing at parts of me and missing all of them. He may have missed all of me because I felt I was ten yards away watching all of this happen, stretching the parts of my body that needed to be there but keeping my abdomen at a safe distance, wanting none of that fighting near me. Maybe that's why he grabbed at space.

The dog strained to get to me but the chain was too short. The man lay there and screamed. The cruel ones are always surprised the way pain hurts; it never ceases to amaze them.

I dropped the stick and asked him if he was okay.

'You attacked me,' he shouted. 'Someone, help me!'

'I'm sorry,' I said. 'I'm sorry.'

'You'll pay for this,' he shouted.

I went home, feeling every step in my right leg. The dog must have wrung himself loose somehow and followed my scent, dragging the chain and the stick it was attached to all the way to my house, because after I reached it he flung himself at the door. I sat on the couch and listened to the chain rattle and the stick crack on the porch as his nails tore strips in the wood, and I thought about the loyalty of dogs who will defend even a cruel master. Or maybe he wanted to live with me now.

And as I sat there bleeding, I figured out that I had changed or else the world had changed. It was one of the two, though it didn't really matter, since one of us did change and it was evidently a done deal. I pushed the graves to one side and made a space where I could put anything that happened to me in the future and observe it before I let it actually happen to me: now I could delay the world and everything in it before it reached me. Now I could find my father in peace.

But I did not think about neighbours and how quickly they dart to a phone if they think they can get you into trouble, especially Mrs Partridge, mother of Emily finger-in-the-jar Partridge, who lived to the right of us, the one whose marathon eyes ran the whole street. The part of me sitting in my new space guessed she probably made straight for the phone at the first sight of the pit bull flinging himself and the stick and the chain at my door, and that she called the police because she wanted to show that she was a responsible person, saying, *And I thought* yak yak *and I wondered* yak yak *and I just need you to know* yak yak *and hope this helps.*

Sick and tired of people. I was getting sick and tired of pushy people always wanting to know things.

Yes, someone called the police and twenty minutes later four of them, two plain clothes and two in uniform, were at the house. The pit bull had a panel of the door in splinters already and they caught the dog in a net. One of them asked me if I'd seen it before.

'That dog,' he pointed.

I followed his finger and shook my head. 'Never.'

They went back to their car and spoke into a radio. Back to the house again. They handcuffed me and sat in the living room with their notebooks, flipping the pages back and forth as if looking for something they hadn't written yet but knew they wanted to write. I'd been seen, they said, and I fitted the description, and what was blood doing on my right sleeve?

'Drying,' I said. I showed the blood to them, pointing out the molecules.

When my mother got back from work, we were all still there and she went pale as they told her I had beaten up a man, the son of a well-respected man in the community, a church leader.

She put her face in her hands. They brought me away and gave her a phone number.

I saw that the judge did not like me. And it got worse after that, probably because I didn't say anything, or because he was friends with the family of the man in question, or so my lawyer thought. I looked at the judge an inch above his eyes in the centre of his forehead, which was also a mistake. And I didn't say anything because I saw my crime in a box on the table in front of me, and I could not put the contents of that box into my head, even if I had opened my head and tried to push everything I had done into it. The pills pushed back. There was no room. I wanted to be sorry, but I couldn't find sorry anywhere. My silence also proved to be a mistake. I was getting sick and tired of people in general now. Sick and tired.

I wondered why my father wasn't in a box either.

The judge put on and removed his glasses.

'You are an unusually detached young man. The person you assaulted had to go to a hospital for treatment, and now, two weeks later, he is receiving treatment for the mental trauma of the beating. I don't believe you're the least bit contrite despite,' he glared at my lawyer, 'the apology your counsel read to the court, which you wrote, according to him. Since you haven't said a word, I can't tell. If I could give you a year, you'd get a year. However, I am restricted by the charges filed,' he glared at the prosecutor, 'to thirty days.' He banged his gavel.

In the gallery, my mother dipped her head to her fingertips.

I went to jail and spent thirty days sitting and eating and sleeping. The other convicts left me alone because they heard why I got sent down and most of them had loved a dog now and then in their lives. Some left me alone because the parts of my body were all different sizes and I couldn't manage them that well and I could get irritable and strike without warning. A man with a big chest who shared my cell showed me a picture of *his* dog and said that if anyone touched me it would be the last time that man touched anything with fingers attached to his body; then he stood up and shouted the same thing down the hall of cell doors. I wa now officially the protector of dogs in the Salt Lake City jail. My mother visited twice the first week, once the second week, and that's when I told her to wait for me at home, that she shouldn't come to a place like this. That I would be fine.

She sat on the other side of the table in the visiting room holding the bag of chocolates she brought me with both hands. 'Are you sure you'll be okay?' she said.

'I have someone looking out for me,' I said. 'No one even looks at me sideways.'

That brought a smile that almost made it up to her eyes: 'The power of prayer.' She sighed and slid the bag across the table. 'I know you'll like those. They're the way you like, Salt.'

I touched the bag and her fingers. She gripped mine tighter than I'd ever known a grip and then placed her other hand on top. It was a blue bag.

I looked inside and saw the pills. So she knew.

'And I told Mr Fargoon you'd be missing this month's session,' she said. 'We'll be different when you get out, you and me both. We can live again. Would you like that?'

I nodded and said, 'A couple of weeks.' I wanted to say her name too – Mary – but I still had a hard time with that since my father called her by her first name and I should say 'Mother' always for that reason, even if she lived to be a hundred and I almost eighty. She looked at me as if trying to find something: she searched my eyes, one to the other as she held me.

When she was gone and I'd counted the pills to figure out how many I had, I remembered I never said how I was sorry for the whole mess. That made me angry with myself. How come I always forgot the important things? And when I was back in my cell I thought of how she looked at me, and then I knew, as I stared at the bed above, what she'd been looking for in my eyes. She wanted me to tell her that what she said − about things being better for us − was true.

After doing the thirty days I went home on the Saturday morning of December 19th, a breezy day where the wind seemed to blow the sun across the sky a bit quicker to get it to the other side. But the season was two days away from the shortest day of the year, and every day felt like a shorter day. The prison bus dropped me off at my house. Since I was the only passenger, the driver talked about his family for the entire twenty-mile drive.

'And say hello to your mother for me,' he said. 'I brought her back the last time after she visited you. She was going my way. Talked about you the whole journey.'

I waved to him and shouted a good wish for his son and walked up the path, noticing three or four newspapers at the door and the curtains drawn completely shut. My mother wasn't home then. My watch said nine o'clock, so she must have gone to work. Ordinary people had lives, and in prison, even for thirty days, I forgot that she would have to work even more now that my father was gone, and I resolved that from this point on it was my turn to work, and if I got a decent job she need not work at all, ever again.

I opened the door, walked up the hallway, left my bag on my bed, went to my mother's room, and then searched the entire house again, but I could not find her, so I poured a bath, soaked my whole body in warm water. Then I thought it would be nice to make the place clean for her, so I swept and washed the floors, opened the windows, washed the dishes, and that's when I discovered she had left a note, which I put away to read after I cleaned up, and then, when I sat down to read her note, I couldn't remember where I'd left the thing.

After I checked my mother's bedroom again I considered the possibility that she had made a mistake about the date I was supposed to be released from prison. Maybe she thought I was due out in sixty days, or ninety days, instead of thirty, and she was staying with relatives to avoid living in an empty house.

I drank some water to wash down a yellow pill.

I watched television into Saturday evening. She did not come home. The note was somewhere in the house and I remembered seeing the word 'late' when I glanced at it after I walked in for the first time. She may have meant she'd be home late from work, even though Mr Swan told me that he had called where she worked downtown and asked them for me. She may have gone to visit relatives in the Salt Lake City area and left the note, and would be back tomorrow or the day after. I was happy that she had company, someone to go to, to talk with. In any case, the house would be nice and clean for her when she got back. I wanted to apologize in person. Because of what I'd done, she'd spent a month on her own.

But shortly after that it came to me that my mother did not have relatives living anywhere near us, so I rechecked the rooms in the house until I knew she wasn't there. All the time, the television droned from the living room. As I passed from room to room I heard something about snow, a forecast for the first winter snowstorm, six inches expected, winds from the north, the city airport bracing for an influx of weekend skiers. Of course: she was with her cousin in Florida; my mother had said she definitely needed a break when she had visited me in prison. The relief spread over me, the kind that replaces a loss with a find.

I lit a fire and walked to my bed room, and as the flames sparked over the wood, I watched from my window as the lake drained the day out of the sky and I scoured the salt bed for lights; but nothing moved out there in miles of ghost white crystals that shone like a weak battery into the rest of the universe.

I grabbed my raincoat and left the house, reached the gate, turned left, and made for the lake, crossing the highway, breathing as deeply as I could, breathing all the salt I could. I must have walked a while because the sky moved with me, wheeling new stars out until the place where all of us had played twelve years ago, guided by the string of lights from the neighbourhood and the mountain on Antelope Island as it rose ahead, a blank triangle cut out of the stars. The salt gleamed at the shore like ice. I removed my shoes and socks and waded out into the cold water with the chill draping my ankles. In a Salt Lake City winter the moon lowers a white straw and sucks every ounce of heat off the face of the world, and the sky had wheeled out that moon, floating thin as a knife cut on the edge of the sky, a slice of it drifting on the water. I felt heat rise from my body like steam and the cold climb into my bones.

The last time I walked in the lake was when my parents went there when my brother was on his way, the four of us splashing around in a warm blue lake of summer. Now my father was dead, so that was three left, my mother had gone to Florida, that brought it temporarily down to two, and my brother never lived at all, which meant we were down to one; but I was not here either – all the lights were off in the world and I was walking in black, and except for the cold in my feet, I had no evidence of being alive myself and could never prove it to anyone, which meant that all those people I called a family who splashed about in summer in a shallow blue lake all those years ago had disappeared off the face of the earth.

Now a few yards offshore, I knelt down and put my head under the water into a different night and waited until it sliced at my lips and forehead like a blade before cutting its ice down to my neck and saturating my shoulders. I opened my eyes in the shock, the only part of me that stirred. All black, brushstrokes of black water, starless black beating of a heart in my ears, my heart, it must have been. My eyes were slits that I squeezed eyesight through.

I looked to where I knew he'd be swimming that time I looked under the water, twelve years before. And then above me I saw a white pill move along the surface, dissolving in waves, and from below, the pale bed of the lake shone back at it. I looked ahead and saw the turbulence coming for me.

'Things may be turning bad. Come back to me, brother,' I said.

SALT 6

I was running a bit low on the blue bag front because I had taken two and sometimes maybe a few more in the jail along with some amphetamine tablets my cellmate gave me when he found me a little dozy a few times. I was a bit hazy on the amphetamines because I was so down when he gave me a big handful to take home with me, and then felt so normal when they balanced out the Xanax that I stopped thinking about them. The combination worked well, I thought. You stay up and down at the same time, somewhere in the middle. Sometimes you have to work at reaching normal. Anyway, I found myself in a position where I needed to take my mother's pills, though only one pillbox of hers was in the closet – she must have taken the other one to Florida.

I slept Saturday night mostly with my eyes open because every time I closed them I saw something swimming toward me in the water, wearing a face I could not see – my brother's, I guessed. Who else could it be? I hadn't called on anyone else.

At dawn on Sunday I lay in bed and let the open windows blow the smell of salt around the room. The salt made everything whiter, and the blue I saw, the blue of the sky at the top of the window, chased in after the salt and tinged the walls, and then the blue and the white and the smell of salt scurried around the floor, blown around and around by the breeze from the lake, the great shallow lake, the lake that lived inside a great desert.

In the kitchen I took her pillbox from the closet and emptied the tablets on to the table, watching carefully as they rolled across the polished surface: I leaned down to smell the wood polish, the lemon brand my mother always liked to use and saw where she'd rubbed it in, the swirls and circles, as if she'd recorded a vinyl record with her work last time she used it; from the evidence of the smell it couldn't have been more than a few days ago that she polished the wood. I folded a cloth and rubbed it anticlockwise to play her back to me, to see if I could hear what she was thinking when she polished, taking one of them along with an amphetamine first. Maybe playing the record of the scratches would show a video of her, maybe it was a DVD and not a record.

I saw how the tablets had rolled into shapes and studied them for an omen and then read the leaflet from the box. Effects, side effects, precautions, antidotes, drawings of chemical properties, and near the top, 'You don't have to feel bad.' And on top, in small type, Lorazepam. Suddenly I was a young boy again, seeing that word, and I reached out my arm and swept the table and watched the pills sail across the kitchen and hit the opposite wall. They fell even though they tried to use their wings to stay in the air, and they scattered across the floor, where I left them, the things that stole my mother little by little.

I stood on one just to hear it die. What a thing to think – killing a pill.

From the floor, in the corners and between the tiles they seemed to taunt me, until an hour later I picked them up and counted them back into the pillbox and put them into the fridge, where I thought they sang to me again, like sirens. We know you want us, Salt, we know you want us.

'Only if you get a hold of me, if I take enough of you,' I said. 'And I won't.'

I imagined a scenario where I tied myself to a chair to stop myself and then flung the chair at the fridge and opened the fridge and took them out again and counted them all in case a couple had run off or were hiding. There's always one. I lined up my mother's Lori's Prams and introduced myself, told them this was a new situation and we all had to get used to it. I have duties for each of you, line up in formation. You, what do you do? And you? 'I don't know,' the pill says, 'same as all the others.' Another pill nods to the one beside it, 'Same as him.' Another pill said that I wasn't what happened to me and I wasn't how I responded to what happened to me, it said, 'You are what you take for what you are and now take me', and I agreed and slipped it into my mouth when it finished speaking, along with one of my cellmate's pills to keep a balance. I knew I was sailing closer to the sirens. The thing was, how close could I get and still stay away?

The pills did not have a lot of room in my head to bother me, because they had lots of company with the questions that were already there. I needed to ask around about my mother, trace her last known movements, even if she'd gone to Florida, or else find that note.

Another voice sounded behind me, in the hall. Not the pills. Definitely not the pills.

'Hello?'

I had not spoken. The voice came from the other side of the door.

'Who is that?' I said.

The slot for the letters in the door opened. 'Is that you?' the voice said.

'Who?' I said.

I bent to the level of the sound, thought I saw a mouth move in the slot.

'Did you find your mother yet?'

'Who are you?' I said.

'Where is your father?'

Whispers coming from down the hall. I felt a breeze around the room, but the doors and windows were closed. A hinge creaked, again from down the hall. Someone was standing at the slot in the door for the letterbox. Whispers floated into the kitchen, and on top of the whispers, or inside them, because I heard words. I heard my name, 'Salt'.

'Where is your mother? Where is your father? Go to Park City, where you will find news of him.'

I swore I saw an angel at my letterbox, its wings crowded to the door while it whispered, an angel, all white, lips moving at the slot. The angel had called me by my name.

I waited at the other end of the hall, wondering what to do. If it was an angel at the door, the game was up. No choice but to go quietly. I'd looked up the word 'angel' a long time ago when I was at school or I asked the teacher to do it for me, and she came back to my desk with a piece of paper and on it was written one word, 'messenger'. 'That's what it means,' she said. I knew that was right because one of them paid me a visit once, twelve years ago, when my brother did not get born. The angel might have been Samuel, the angel of Tuesday and death, or Cassiel, the angel of Saturday and solitude. Yes, I think it was one of those two that dropped by one day twelve years before and stuck his head in my room and looked at me straight in the eye and gave me a message. He said, 'Your brother is dead. He will never be alive. He had to come with me. I'm just telling you so you'll know. I know your mother told you about me, how I took your brother, now I'm telling you. And one day I'll be back for you.'

Well, now he was back. But I wasn't a young boy anymore, so be ready for a fight, angel.

As I waited in the hall I wondered why angels didn't seem to have any emotions, why they carried messages from one world to another without a world of their own. Perhaps angels did not know what they were, that they were lost. If so *this* one wasn't lost.

'What do you know about my father? Just one second,' and I ran for the door.

The voice did not wait: 'Where is your father. Where is your mother? Doesn't that bother you?'

I reached the door. No one there. I rushed to the gate. Nothing on either side all the way down the pavement. A breeze blew some white shirts from a top floor window across the street.

It was time to go back to the lake to check for my brother.

I put one raincoat over another, a medium and extra large, with the medium stretched over the large one, and walked to the lake shore, this time with a pair of goggles, like divers used, and bent under the surface to see if there was any progress. Water swilled in, so I fastened the goggles better around my head and turned to a child who was walking with her parents, but her mother hustled her off quickly, saying 'Leave the man alone', and bundled her off with the kite that struggled to get away too. I don't blame you, kite, I said. I'd be at the end of my rope if I were you listening to people all day saying do this, that, let's do this, see child what I'm doing now. Child must be out of her mind too. People should never say anything. Hearing and touching off the list too. Too much of the world crowding into you. Already too full in here, do you mind? I have enough information, I'm fine. I needed one sense: smell. Live like flowers stuck to the side of a hill in a breeze, a bit of clay, a bit of sun. Get away from me. Everyone. Get away for ever. Do it now. Understand what I'm meaning. I have had enough.

I kneeled again in two feet of water and smashed my face into the lake with my eyes wide open and my hands gripping the goggles to keep the seal. The white mattress bed, bluer water, calm but over there, ahead, ten yards, no more, limbs thrashing the water into currents. 'Come on,' I said to the disturbance, you're closer now, I am here, 'you're doing well to get this far, I know how difficult it must be, keep trying, move through the water, make it this time, don't stop, brother, don't give up and let yourself float away, hold your breath, hold your breath, brother, and come back to me.'

I promised I'd be back the next day and walked a trail of drops back to the house. The neighbours, of course, watched with their mouths open and shook their heads as

if something was caught inside their skulls that they could-
n't get out no matter how hard they tried. *Can't you get it
out*, I wanted to say to them. Is it bothering you that much,
is it? My options were limited in asking them for help.
After what happened to the Simmons family I did not visit
the people on our street any more because they turned
away in a crisis, and I didn't much care for that. Now I had
gotten a little less caring in a much bigger way. I think I
may have actually said something to some people after that
family disappeared with nothing but what fitted into their
car, and I think I may have said it loudly to quite a few
people in the supermarket one day, called them a bunch of
bastards, and I think the police were called and I was
'escorted' out. The sergeant at the desk was nice and said
he understood but that I should get some help.

There was no time for pride. When I got back to the
house I combed my hair and straightened my raincoats and
set out along the street for the houses of my neighbours.
The wide concrete street had some cracks in it through
which grass grew in clumps, shining green against the sun.
It was nice to see the streets as if for the first time, with
bigger and better-kept houses, greener lawns, nicer cars
and better-dressed children; yes, the streets were as new,
wider and whiter and blowing with salt. The area was
improving with every passing day. I'd never noticed how
wide the streets were before, the *dramatic* improvement in
the view from one end of the street to the other. The
world was improving with every passing day.

I saw my hand – bigger than it ever was and floating in
front of me somewhere attached to the rest of me, like on
a space walk, caused by the pills, I knew – I saw my hand

rise up in front of my eyes and into a fist and make contact three times with the door of the Partridge family, of 23 Lake View Drive, two doors to the right of our house. It seemed a good idea to ask if they knew anything that might help.

The door opened to the face of the younger Partridge, hand-in-the-jar Partridge, thirteen years old.

'Hello, Emily,' I said. Somewhere, I knew it was my voice sounding from somewhere near my head, from the area of my right ear. *Come closer, voice.* Stay inside my tongue, where you were born. I hauled it back into me with a string. I'd have to cut back on the prams and I had this image then of nine women walking – as many as fit across the width of my mind's eye – pushing their prams, and when I wnt to look at the babies I saw the word *Alphie* written on the pillons instead.

Emily looked over my shoulder, left and right, then back to me, hand on the door as if ready to slam it at a moment's notice.

'Hello,' she said in half a question, half a statement.

'I was wondering if I could come in for a minute,' I said. 'I have something to ask you.'

She chewed her gum and her eyes went blank. 'What is it?' she said, taking a step back, door wavering in her hand.

I said, 'I'm actually looking for my mother and I wondered if you knew where she was. I think she's in Florida but I want to rule out that she might be lost.'

More chewing. 'No.'

'Are you sure?'

'How would I know?' Chewing louder.

'That's what I'm asking, Emily.' As I said that I realized

she looked so far away because I was still wearing the goggles. I removed them.

She smiled. 'I heard you were dragged off her, and you were mean to my parents.'

'Dragged off who—?' Parts of me wanted to leave and go for different walks while I spoke with Emily but I gripped them harder than I did the goggles. 'What dragged, where are you talking about?'

'*You* know,' she sneered. 'Saying you were sorry, you were sorry, and you were really mean – what you said to my parents – and you never said sorry to us, well, you got your own sorry back now, didn't you?'

The door slammed shut.

'You know—' I said and banged on it once more, but she didn't open it again.

'Someone knows something!' I rattled the handle, but someone locked the door and I heard footsteps. A curtain twitched as I closed the gate behind me. A curtain twitching meant the house had something in its eye.

I arrived back at the house with a headache and a dry tongue. That didn't stop me calling my mother's name. An answer came from down the hall, I thought one did, so I checked her room, but the bed was unmade and her slippers waited on the floor. Maybe tomorrow morning I would wake and find her, lying in bed, or in the kitchen, making coffee, back from her relatives. First would be the relief, the chest relaxing after all that shallow breathing all day, the same panic I had when I was in prison, the panic I kept from her when she visited, and then, when I see it's really her and that it was all a time mix-up, I ask her where she's been and she explains everything – that she left a note, didn't I get it? *I lost it*, I say. So many pieces of paper everywhere. She laughs and we decide plans for the rest of our lives. New lives. Restaurants, trips, she tells me about how she grew up, about her own parents, things we'd never talked about before, and I was not going to let that happen again, not talking about important things, because my father died before we said those things, and no, no, never that mistake again. I sigh the rest of the fear out of me and breathe joy back in with an even deeper breath. We laugh, she strokes my hair, and I go out and get a job and find friends and live a normal life. That was the plan if I found her here tomorrow or if she found me.

I was still in her room when I heard the voice again calling my name. Keep talking, I said to myself, and rummaged through the sheets, lifted the carpet, checked behind the door. Keep talking and I'll follow your voice and find you. I traced the voice to the pillbox in the kitchen closet and emptied the pills out and I ate the one that seemed to be calling me. Then it went quiet after I swallowed it. No, it didn't have a whole lot to say then. My stomach very briefly floated off and I had to run after it to get it back. I was running close to losing my body: a dangerous game, this.

It was only noon on Sunday, so I had plenty of time for another visit to one of my fellow citizens, another set of questions that might explain my mother's absence or lead to her.

This time I decided to turn left out the gate, since right didn't seem to be a good turn on this street. I splashed water on my face and left the house and found myself one door to the left, at 20 Lake View Drive, where Mr Swan had lived on his own for the seven years since Mrs Swan passed on. I knocked on his door and waited for a minute or two until the door opened and a smile appeared, because the poor man was happy to get a visit from anyone, and that's the way he opened the door, full of expectation, but when his watery eyes saw it was me, he leaned heavier on his cane and pulled the hem of his sweater down as if preparing for a sudden ordeal against which he had no defence.

'Hello, Mr Swan.'

'Good, good afternoon.' As with Emily, he also looked over my shoulder, but his eyes weren't that good and the world behind my shoulder probably swam with foggy shapes.

'I was wondering if I could come in for a minute,' I said.

He looked down like a man figuring out a very complicated road sign.

'Yes.' He walked ahead of me but switched the cane to his left hand and kept to the right wall of his hallway.

'Thanks, Mr Swan, I won't be long.'

We proceeded along the hallway and entered a room full of very green plants and a single white table with two chairs, on top of which another plant draped its shoots and leaves. He sat carefully, his eyes fixed on me. After he was comfortable, I said, 'I was hoping you might have seen my mother in the last couple of days.'

He shook his head.

'If there's anything at all you might know,' I said.

He shook his head so hard his cheeks wobbled and some spit splintered his lower lip.

'Did you see my mother this week?'

'I last saw her Monday, before you, you know.'

'Got back?'

'Yes.'

'What was she doing when you saw her?'

'She was coming home from work, I think. She went for a walk out there.' He pointed to the lake. 'She walked in her work clothes. Didn't seem cold but it was cold, you know. I had to turn the heat up. She must have been cold in those clothes, looked distracted.'

He coughed and reached for something that wasn't on the table, then brought that hand back to the other, clasping them together on the hook of the cane. He was at an age when he may have meant to continue and forgot. I watched the television flicker behind him with an image of two jets taking off from an aircraft carrier. Through his arms and the walking stick, I saw a reporter say, 'Today, fear grips the nation.' The next image showed three men wearing black ski masks crouching with rifles. A man with a microphone and a tie said, 'Where are the terrorists hiding?'

As Mr Swan dabbed his lip with a hanky, the reporter turned into an advertisement showing a concerned family sitting close together looking at a television:

'Experiencing fearful thoughts? Is your child suffering the effects of an increasingly dangerous and unpredictable world? Talk to your doctor about Serenax.'

I made a note. That was a new one. Must not be a Pharmalak product or I'd have been on to it already. Good friends with the pharmacist at Pharmalak now.

Mr Swan looked at me and tried to smile. I smiled for

him and stood and thanked him, and then he made to get up too. I told him to stay where he was. As I walked down his hallway I glanced back and saw that he was slumped in his chair watching a man on the television being searched by a soldier. Mr Swan again reached for something that wasn't on the table.

It must be tea or coffee, I thought. I should make him some because after all he was good enough to say something to me. So I went to his kitchen and saw in a line on the countertop the ten or twelve pillboxes, a pill crusher, a pink pill tray separated into the days of the week, and the number of the pharmacy. I boiled the water and found instant coffee in the closet. As I rounded the corner into the living room holding his cup, I saw two people debating on television. The woman said:

'We have to support the war—'

The man on the television shook his head and began to say something as she rose above his words with louder words like a ship climbing up a wave. Mr Swan sat still. I placed the cup to his right, on the table, and walked away, hoping he was okay and that the cup would find his fingers when he reached again. Down the hall I heard a word from the television show:

'Terror—'

I closed the door behind me and felt the sun on my forehead; the blue water before me creased like a fingerprint under the breeze. I saw fear stretched out along the horizon in a line-up, or it might have been a trick of the light. Two or three pieces of shrapnel flew past me and landed on a tree, and then they sang, and I saw that they were birds. I walked the few yards to my own door, my hands shaking. So nothing from Mr Swan. Nothing from the Partridges. But a file had been opened somewhere and someone knew something.

At home, predictably of course, the pills still sounded as if they were shouting, and predictably in the kitchen, so I took another one to shut them all up and washed it down with water and put the rest of them in a plastic bag and zipped it shut and put it into the icebox in the fridge. Shout all you want now, I said. *I'm not going to allow you to run the show.*

I checked the time. Two o'clock. Time to go out and buy some coffee, wake myself up, felt groggy because I didn't sleep well with my eyes open most of the night. As I closed the front door of the house I was so tired I wondered if this was like being dead, and then I got to thinking what it would be like to be dead for a day; since I already felt that way, acting dead wouldn't be such a hard thing to do. I read once that you should live life as though you were already dead. Spend a night sleeping in a coffin, realize what you think now that you are dead and can't change anything, then wake up and live the way you were supposed to in the first place.

So I turned right at the gate and walked past number 23, where Mr. Partridge was bent over a hose in his garden, his back turned to me. Ah, so the Partridges were out of the house with the sore eye. He looked up, made an attempt to wave, and caught himself, but because he couldn't have waved at me, since I was dead, I walked on without acknowledging him, even though he was the nicest of the Partridges and I wanted to turn back and say hello to him since I knew he was probably watching me and waiting for me to say hello back. I walked to the corner of the block and did not wave at the child who carried her tricycle out of my way. But she smiled because I often gave her things out of my pocket, a coin, or some chocolate when I had it to give. Today, however, I was dead, and dead people don't hand out chocolate.

When I bought soap and coffee at the supermarket I did not say hello back to the cashier who went out of her way to make eye contact with me. I think she must have been looking at someone behind me, because, of course, I was in fact dead on that particular day and was completely invisible. If I weren't dead I would have asked her how Andy Simmons was doing now that the photo of little Andy and the jar had been taken away and replaced with a collection jar for the Kent Animal Shelter.

I went home and saw some mail addressed to me, which I ignored, since dead people had no business reading letters. When the telephone rang I picked it up in case it was someone looking for someone else, or my mother calling. Someone asked for me. I hung up, since talking while dead was out of the question. I was able to watch television, however, as the dead can most likely see and hear; that is, if they survive being dead and can hear and see. An hour went by like a numb patch of skin, not surprising, since being dead you have no body, and therefore there's nothing to feel.

I must have fallen asleep in my dad's armchair, and when I woke, I found I was alive again. I put my hands down along my body while looking at the ceiling and felt a chest, hips, a thigh. Yes, I had a body and a headache to prove it. I switched on the light because it was dark outside, after four o'clock, and walked down the hall and knocked at my mother's door, three times and slowly, in case she was tired from all the travelling over the weekend. She did not answer, and when I opened her door, I saw the unmade bed.

Still no mother.

An undisturbed silence, deeper than recent silence, like dust. And as I thought about it while I made coffee, no word from the neighbours either. One of them saw something. The Partridges, for instance. The mother always had a head stuck to the window. A symptom of trouble in your life is when neighbours disappear.

Three loud knocks on the front door. *Ah, but I'm ready for you this time.* I crept up so the voice wouldn't hear me coming this time and yanked it open. The police sergeant from the local station stood back, the same man who came for me in the supermarket.

'Hello, Salt,' he said.

'Hello, Sergeant.'

'Are you okay?' he said.

'I'm okay.' Maybe I could live as an echo.

'I heard from Mr Swan today,' he said.

'You heard from Mr Swan today?'

'Yes, but he just mentioned that you called by his place this morning and he was surprised when he found the coffee you made for him.'

The sergeant slipped his card into my hand and I watched him drive away along the empty street. Before he did drive off, however, he asked me not to bother the neighbours again. There had been calls to the station, he said. You mean Mr Swan, I said. No, other calls too, he said. I wonder who that might have been, I said. He said that he didn't want to say, and that it didn't matter anyway, since I wouldn't be calling on the neighbours any more, was that right?

I said, 'Yes, I won't bother the Partridges any more so they won't have to call you any more.'

'Are you all right?' he said, looking at me carefully.

I gripped the door and nodded.

After he was gone, I had to fix the two raincoats so they fit better because they were drying and getting tighter on me, especially the smaller one. I finally pulled them off from my body and flapped them while bending forward at my bedroom window, letting some fresh air in. Back in the kitchen, above the steam of the coffee cup, I watched the evening news. The announcer said, 'And that's the news from abroad. And now this important message.' The scene switched to a woman driving a convertible along a coastal highway, looked like a fine early morning or late evening. The camera swung to a close side profile. She was smiling, her hair blowing behind her, her scarf loose about her neck. A word appeared in white at the bottom right corner of the screen and a voice said, 'Get your life back with Elevax.'

Must try that, I said. This is good. One pill says I don't have to feel bad, and another pill says I can get my life back. That's not damn bad for only a couple of pills.

I went to the bathroom and saw my face, felt it with my fingers, saw the beard. Last time I looked in the mirror I was clean-shaven. Good thing I didn't have to go to work today, no regular work, not since my dad died, some jobs sweeping floors and stacking things in industrial yards, that was all. Before my dad died I was going to go to college.

But that was then. The now was in the mirror, before me. The future was somewhere else and currently unavailable.

I held a new razor blade and dragged it across my right cheek and felt the tug of the whiskers back until a few snapped away. To make it easier I rubbed soap in my hands and added water until it foamed a little and then spread it across the beard. The mirror steamed a little with the hot water, but I could see the beard disappear in strips as I dragged the blade over my face. I splashed water and dried off with a towel. Now that I was presentable again, I could go downtown and find out if my mother was at work. A long shot. The phone call earlier I think was from her.

At close to five o'clock I rode the train to the city centre and walked three blocks to her building. I walked up to the glass front and the large doors and through another set of circling doors and into the lobby, where a man moved quickly out from behind a desk.

'Can I help you?'

'Yes,' I said, relieved that someone was offering to do something. He stood before me, his shoulders wide.

I said, 'I was hoping to go upstairs to where my mother works and see if she's there today.'

'And your mother is?'

'Missing. She's been missing.'

I could see a hand inside his eyes pull a string and a bulb light up. He moved an arm out to his side. 'Sit here, please, and we'll have someone come see you.'

'Okay.' I walked to the line of chairs in the lobby. Some people looked me up and down, and then I looked myself up and down and saw that I was still wearing the two raincoats and the boots I'd slept in. In no time at all, two men wearing strong aftershave and suits walked across the marble lobby floor. One of them reached into his pocket and held a tissue to me.

'You're bleeding,' he smiled.

I wiped my face and saw the line of blood. The other man sat beside me.

'And you're Salt, Mary's son?'

'Yes, I came to find her.'

They exchanged a glance, the type who stay calm and don't let you know what they're thinking, and I knew I shouldn't move from where I was. The one beside me asked me some questions about when I'd seen her last, and I said in prison, that she hadn't been able to visit me often because of work. He nodded. The other man left and came back with a bottle of water and another tissue. I wiped my face again and drank some water. I didn't notice the third person until his hand touched my shoulder and I looked into his eyes, the sergeant's eyes.

He said, 'Salt, let's go. Your mother isn't here. It's a Sunday and people aren't working today.'

I rose with the help of a firm grip. The sergeant thanked the two men and walked me through the large circling glass doors and then out the main front door and into the sunlight. He let go once we were outside and opened the door of his patrol car.

'I'll drive you home,' he said. We drove in silence, except for the radio that cackled every few seconds, and he dropped me off at my house, bringing me to the door where he shook my hand and asked me not to go down-town again until the situation with my mother had been resolved. He insisted that I not go downtown. Said that he didn't want to have to come to get me again. That I would not want that. And no more visits to anyone. I agreed to everything because I could see he was upset.

Once I entered the house, the noise from the television accompanied me along the hall back to the living room. I sat in my father's armchair watching Humphrey Bogart in *The Big Sleep*. The smell of the cigarettes he always smoked into the evening rose off the fabric. How strange it was that I was sitting there, smelling what my father had breathed out, a part of him still living in the fabric, and now in me. I sat in the dark and let the light from the television brighten the room.

The clock circled to nine o'clock.

I go up and checked the hall for voices, then moved carefully along it to the kitchen, where I made coffee in the dark in case anyone was watching. I sat at the table and held the coffee close to my face. The steam wet my nose and forehead, yet I felt nothing, as if my mind had emptied everything out of itself and forgotten to put something back. My stomach boiled with every second. I raised the mug to my lips and left it there, inside the upper lip, just where it burned, so that I would feel the pain and wake up and be Salt again, Salt at home, Salt at school, Salt at college. But I felt none of those things; and although the pain did come, it registered a few feet away from me, near the painting of the sea above the kitchen table. *Come back, pain*, I thought. And be with me. I want to feel you inside me, not over there. But the pain stayed where it was. It said, *I'm sorry, but I don't know who you are*. The steam made my eyes tear up; still I did not cry. The tears, I guessed, may have thought they were mine, from me, but when they saw the face under them as they left my eyes, they must have refused to fall on my face, since it was a strange face, and that is why I did not cry. My hands still shook, but I knew they shook because they belonged to someone else and because they wanted that person back.

The coffee on my tongue. I floated in one big heartbeat. Perhaps it was the Partridges who spoke at the door earlier, the young one, about what I did with my mother or whatever the way it was said was. Yes, she said something and ran off. Little bitch.

So I ran to her house and banged on the door, asking why she'd said those things. They did not come to the door, but I heard them calling for me to go away, that they were calling the police. I went back to my house and sat in the kitchen. After a few minutes I heard yet another voice coming down the hall, calling my name. It might have been the sergeant. I kept quiet until he went away, which was a long time.

At ten o'clock I opened the icebox and checked to see if the pills were saying anything. They didn't have a whole lot to say, really, since I had consumed quite enough of them already. Their voices were frozen in their throats. If I did nothing for a day those throats would open again and shriek for food like little birds or more dangerous things, the sirens that addicts hear all day long. Not for me. I put one on my tongue to warm it up, but it slipped down my throat the first chance it got. I put the rest back in the bag and covered them with more ice to keep them fresh.

When I was tired enough I went to my bedroom and sat at the window and put back on the two raincoats as well as three pairs of socks, waiting for the lights. No, wait, the lights were gone, I forgot. It had been a while. I wanted to cry and couldn't because somehow my organs were all mixed up. The house pulled at me with a hollow sound as if the rooms were fingers groping at me, telling me to come back and live in each of them and be happy to be alone, since that was my lot. I answered that the house must think it was talking to my father, that my father was gone and it shouldn't be wasting its time talking to me. And it answered back that it knew my father was gone and it knew very well that it was talking to me. The house said it felt alone and I was the only one around. I was on my own, the house said, though my father, the house said, knew it from a much earlier age that being alone was going to last for the rest of his life, just as I would, and that I should just turn around and go back into the rooms and live as my father did, a quiet man in a quiet life.

I don't know why, but I felt as clear as a bell in wintertime, and for a short while it was nice until the loneliness came back like two hard planks, one front and one back, nailed to each other through my stomach.

Maybe the house had turned into something else while I watched the lake bed. Maybe the rooms had switched places with each other, and my mother's bedroom was now the living room, and the bathroom was the kitchen. Maybe all the rooms were lined up outside my room and there was no home at all any more, just rooms with nobody in them and they all wanted me to visit them. 'No,' the house said, and this showed me that it was obviously listening in to my thoughts – No, we want you to visit just one room.

'You know the one.'

I whirled around. 'I don't know any such thing about what room you are referring to.'

I was so tired that dreams and wakefulness were talking to each other, blending in a stew. I needed to rest. When I turned back to the window, I saw a light out on the high-way and put both hands to the glass in hope. My mother driving back from Florida. But it moved too fast, and was joined by another. A car sped by. I felt so tired. Anyway, our car was parked in the driveway.

But sleep got delayed on the way to my body. I think it ran into a plastic bag of pills in the icebox, the ones I had to check on after I had the conversation with the rest of the house. When I counted them before putting them back there was one pill less than when I took them out of the icebox. I think because it got into my mouth. I sent an amphetamine after it for company, that's what stopped me from sleeping I'll bet.

It was close to midnight.

SALT 7

One o'clock and all is well.

There's a point at which sleep doesn't matter. Your body drifts toward that point for a few hours and when it reaches it, your mind floats off after your body, they touch briefly and lose contact, and then your senses float off in different directions, some swirling in eddies, others going headlong for the waterfall. Left behind, you look with the last sense left, your sight, and watch them evaporate, and if all goes well, you close your eyes.

It occurred to me that my mother wasn't gone at all. I wondered if it was possible to live in a house with another person and never see her. Two people can have different schedules. One leaves for work, the other arrives home two minutes later; they just miss each other. Messages on the telephone, notes on the table, food left in the fridge, that's how they make contact. And when at work, they each get lost in a world with its own sense of time, and after work, they meet with their colleagues for dinner or drinks, and when they get back home, the other person who lives there is out for a walk or meeting with friends, and it goes on like this for days or weeks. You could live with someone and go days without actually meeting them. I had heard of such couples, especially on our street, where people had to work so much, and I determined to check my mother's bedroom at regular intervals to see if she was sleeping there and I also came up with the following strategy: to stick both arms out and touch the walls while I walked along corridors so I'd brush against her if she was passing and we didn't notice each other.

I played another film and watched it every time I passed the living room. The rest of the plot I picked up through the dialogue, though it was a bit strange missing parts where a lot was happening. After a while I heard a slapping sound that didn't seem to come from the film. I walked back to the living-room door. Slapping sound. I walked to the letterbox. Slapping sound. But as I walked again the slapping resumed, and that's when I saw the paper sticking to my shoe. There were some papers on the floor, it's true, and this one flapped around enough to make me notice it. I pulled it off my shoe.

No, two pages, white paper filled with writing, small, thin, spidery, careful letters, and I thought it might be from my mother, or a note someone left in the house for me, because I didn't remember the pages being there when I left. I brought them to the kitchen table, where I sat and read:

One day I stood in the bathroom in front of the mirror and decided to look for the grief inside of me. I had been feeling it for so long and thought it must be somewhere on top of my stomach. I felt under my ribs just in case. No grief there, no bumps. So I put my hands inside my skin and felt around, took out one organ at a time and lined them up around the sink: the liver, the stomach, wrapped neatly, the kidneys, the heart. Nothing.

I heard a voice say the words while I read them, as if an echo attached itself to the letters in advance and let loose when my eye hit the word. Maybe that's what memory is: an echo and a magnet. The strangest thing. I turned to the next page.

Maybe it dodged behind my liver when I put it back. Now it sat on my stomach, trampling around along my blood and making me tired all the time. Must be stuffing paper into the pipes of my senses to keep out the draught or to seal itself in, because I don't smell or taste things as well as before. Or maybe it blocked them up because it wants the silence and wants to live undisturbed, even move in some furniture, put its own handmade soap in the bathroom with fragrance of gone and forgotten. When you wipe it across your face, you forget large parts of your body. When that soap covers your face, people no longer see the man you were. The skin is the same, the eyes, the eyebrows, the mouth, but the man is gone. It has lots of things it likes to hoard for itself. Then I put them back until I was in one piece again.

That was all the writing, though there was more some-where on another page, you could tell by the sentences the way they were going. I held the strange note and wondered who left it there, maybe the voice that spoke through the letterbox also dropped off this note. I concluded that my own father must have used that disappearing soap. So much of his life he seemed a stranger even to himself, but certainly to others. And the things grief liked to keep for itself? My father's face, for instance. I couldn't find it anywhere. I should have it. I had it last night in my mind's eye and then it faded. That must have been the hand of grief that stole it, pulling his face away, down to its room in my body, to a closet in its room, to a sheaf of papers in that closet, the papers pinned under a stone.

Maybe the missing page was on the floor. There were a lot of them on the floor.

Then from the fridge behind me drifted the voices of the pills, the sirens in the refrigerator. They said that if I took more of them I wouldn't get any more notes like that and that I wouldn't feel bad any more and that I'd be free of my parents for ever. I didn't have to feel bad, remember? they said. And why did you pick it up to read it when the same energy could have been spent opening the refrigerator door and taking one of us? Can you answer us that?

I'd heard enough and opened the fridge and carried the pills into my mother's room and left the bag on her bed. Remember her? I said, and closed the door. Talk all you want now. She's heard it before. Before I left them, though, I picked another one out of the bag, put it on my tongue and forgot about it, but I'm sure that sooner or later it found its own way down.

The third page I found was lying in the doorway to the living room. I saw my hand reach down for it and turn it to the writing on the other side. Same handwriting, same type of paper. This one I read in the light of the television:

One day you wake and a man's voice is silent. If the
silent voice is not yours, you can proceed through the
house to find who owns it by going to the places you
once heard talking or laughter. You can look first in
the hallway and then one room at a time. Then you
search near objects, because silence lives in objects too.

Once you might have heard the missing voice
come from an armchair or speak under a lamp, but
now they represent a voice that is gone. Here is a
partial list of other objects that can represent silence:
rings, music, doorways, chairs, photographs, medals,
books, paths, woods, lakes, bridges, shoes. You
might hear the person you lost in all of those.

At the bottom of the page I read, 'Nemocot 10 mg,
once per day, dispense as written.'

I put that note with the other one I'd stuffed into my raincoat pocket. Let's see: a person takes out his organs and looks
for silence in the furniture of a house; that note was best kept
in my bedroom in case anyone snooping around read it. I
was walking out of the living room to put them there when
I saw a fourth page at the front door, like a trail leading me
out of the house, and I looked to the ceiling in case they
were dropping out of the sky, but the roof was still there.

You never have to lose anyone. You can store them
for ever on photos, on voice recorders, on paper.
You can wrap them in plastic, in boxes, you can
place them in a deep freeze and thaw them out
when you want to see or hear them again. They will
dance again for you on video, smile again for you in

photographs, speak to you one more time on tape.
You can even save your own childhood, play back
your earliest moments, smiles, walks, your cut knee,
a lost toy. You can be with people long gone, friends
who changed without warning.

I remembered how my father became what he smoked:
he had a voice like a pack of cigarettes. He stopped smoking a few years before he died, but it was too late. The
smoke liked his body so much that it filled out little holes
for itself and even ate away part of his lungs to stop him
breathing too much fresh air. He gasped for breath with
every step but would not stop trying to walk and remain
active, and only when his heart gave out did he stop, and
then it was for ever. I read the rest of the note:

Maybe it's better to have nothing at all of those who
are gone. Face the loss with the loss of all faces. No
eyes, no beach, no smiles, no weddings, no births.
Take everything of those departed – the ring, the
scarf, the gloves, the perfume bottle, that voice on
the tape, the letters, the shopping list you found in a
drawer – all the things you have of your parents, take
them all and burn them. Burn them. Now the only
life they'll have is the one they live in you. Could
you bear doing that?

And underneath, 'Response improving, continue current meds.' The page floated like water in my hands and I
folded it and stuffed it in with the other two.
When my mother and I did meet again, I hoped I

would recognize her. We'd never been apart for this long, and I had never committed her face to memory, really to memory. There must have been times when I talked to her without looking, listened to her without looking, handed her letters or breakfast without looking, said goodbye without looking. I never snapped pictures, we weren't that kind of family. Now that she was missing, I could not be sure what she really looked like, could not describe her features to a stranger, and the trouble was that if I went to the police station to enquire after her, the police officer might ask me for a description, a description of my own mother. I resolved to find photographs of her and carry them with me, so that I could check the faces I met against the photographs. To do this, however, I would have to search her bedroom or the kitchen closets, where she always put keepsakes and things like photographs. There was nothing else for it, I was going to have to look in every nook and cranny, every pocket and space, every shelf. Her face was lost. Not to worry, she'd be back presently. She had gone off visiting someone in Florida a couple of months ago, after my dad died, for a long week-end. She had a relative there, a cousin who took good care of her. She told me. Must be with her again. Those were most likely all the messages on the phone for me, that she was coming back in thirty, sixty, ninety days, she'd be that late, what was on the note she left. Okay, enough already. She's recovering in her own way and that will be the right way.

I think she did call yesterday. Said she was doing fine.

Some people blow through your life like a page in a windy garden; you look around and the page is already two gardens down and you wonder where it went all of a sudden and if you'll ever read it again.

What if the police said they needed to know what my mother sounded like? I knew the sound of my mother's voice, been hearing it since birth, but I didn't have a tape recording of it or a film on which she spoke. I could recover how she spoke by repeating words she said often, this word soft, that vowel low, this type of laugh. It was as simple as finding something she wrote and thinking of her saying it, imagining the hand that wrote it, the table she sat at, and when I had all the parts in place, I could put them back together and recreate her. But the truth was that I did not have the sound of her voice anywhere.

Her voice was lost.

I did find two photographs of my mother in the kitchen closet. The first photo was no good as a means of identification. She looked about fifteen years old and sat in the middle of a group of other boys and girls in what looked like a meadow. She wore long hair, and because she sat in the middle and in the front row, I guessed she was very popular.

In the other photo she was older, maybe twenty-one, and she lay at a river's edge with a couple of girls and some young men dressed in neat shirts and white pants, one of whom carried a mandolin. They looked happy, and since the photograph was black and white, as if they lived in another age, in an easier time to be alive. But no one would recognize my mother from that photograph, since it was now thirty years old. I also found a box under her bed that contained the following: a plastic brown wallet; a woven basket; a belt; an envelope with a lock of my hair snipped on my first birthday; a letter from her aunt; a photograph of her own mother.

Two o'clock in the morning.

I walked to the window and leaned my face on my hands and knew I could not sleep. I was so tired that sleep itself was no longer any good. Somehow, tiredness had taken hold of me and would not be moved along or disposed of by closing my eyes, not for hours, not for days. Tiredness was here to stay. I looked out at the salt flats, the chalk wilderness to the west and heard the wind carry the smell across the night. Even the stars were hiding. I thought that if I breathed hard enough, I could draw the dark itself into me. But if the dark entered me, it would have company too. So I lit a candle to light my face and prove to the world that Salt was alive tonight.

Tomorrow was the shortest day of the year, and I watched the city's lights spread like a broken yellow vase up the mountainside and peter out into the black. I'd go to the doctor in those mountains tomorrow. I lay my forehead on the sill, and when I woke a couple of hours later, someone had cleared the clouds away and thrown a handful of stars across the surface of the lake.

Four o'clock in the morning.

I passed under the bulb in the hall and the noisy snow on the television before checking to see how the pills were doing in the bedroom. I had counted wrong the last time, had counted one too many.

I drank the pill down with a cup of water and reached the front door and did not feel my feet step down to the bicycle lying against the fence, and as I wheeled it out the

gate, I looked back to my bedroom window and the curtain blowing out into the sky. I saw the young boy who
used to sit at the window looking for the lights, saw his
young face hoping for his brother to come back, and I told
him that it wouldn't be long now.

I walked the bicycle out on to the salt flats, then ran out
on to them, threw a leg over the saddle and cycled fiercely
to keep warm. I was wearing the black raincoats and sunglasses and didn't have a light on the bike, drawing circles
and watching for lights. On the road, someone passed and
blew a horn because he nearly hit me when I crossed the
highway because he didn't know how to drive in a straight
line. A single light gleamed on a hillside and disappeared.
The tyres rasped on the salt as I turned a circle and headed
further out, gaining speed, faster and faster till my raincoats
flapped out to both sides like wings. In the silence I
thought the shadows themselves rustled; I thought I saw the
part of a face, a wisp of white. Another light off to the
right. I cycled faster, closing my eyes because I did not
have to see what was not there, only salt, nothing else.
When I reached a small hill I parked the bike and sat on the
slope. The pages I pulled from my inside pocket were different from the ones I'd read. I had found them mostly by
the door on the way out the house and picked them up,
unfolded the pages and sifted through them. The moon was
out from behind the clouds, strong as a flashlight on the
words.

A phrase I heard once: my father lived an
unobserved life. No one saw him when he dressed
for the day, undressed for bed, listened to the radio,

read a book, went for a walk. No one saw him
watch television, light a fire, rub the cat's head, fall
asleep in the armchair. Not even someone in a room
at the other end of the house. No one saw him lose
his friends to bad stomachs and bad hearts. No one
saw his friends grow thinner and fewer than his
fingers. No one saw him rush to the phone when it
rang, even at 3 a.m., to hear a voice.

The same spidery writing as the previous notes, the slant,
the precision. While all the others I'd found had a clean
edge, the next one had a rip that curved into the writing as
if someone had torn it up. Holding it together, I sat down
to read it through the steam of my breathing.

A father is a voice. You heard it from your earliest
moments along with another voice that kept you
content and warm. When you were older, his voice
closed any distance with a word. A father is a hand
that held you close, and when you took your first
steps, you stumbled your first journey alone to that
hand. A father is a river. He never carried you inside
his body, and so when he held you for the first time,
you flowed straight to his own father.

More notes written at the bottom of the page,
'*Discontinue trial*'. And then more writing under that:
    'Aren't you listening to me? None of this is going to
work. No cure except time, I'm telling you, time. It will
outlast you, outstare you, outlive you. No cure for this
because we're made of time, built into time, time, time. We

do our time, can't you hear me? Nothing to take but time.'

As I slipped along the salt I felt the moon graze my arm like a cold finger, a wet light that cooled on its way down through the atmosphere where I saw pills, thousands of pills, scattered across the sky. I was in the land of pills. I could have reached my fingers up and into that pile and tasted what health is when you can fix it, just like that. Live longer, live cleaner, live happier, live without affliction, live in the land of youth, island of the eternal young. Live without jealousy and spite and regret. Be blissful all the time. Cancel out the rage and the strange.

The sky stood with its own large round white pill in its hand up there, framed in the valley. I could hold it in my fingertips and taste it, something to make me feel better, or even feel. I just wanted to feel something. But too many of my mother's and Fargoon's pills had found their way into me.

Wind cleared the sky of clouds, and I saw the lights in the sky were gone. Then I saw another white page rise above the horizon in the east. Dawn. I swear I heard the dawn talking to me:

'Go to the cemetery this evening. Your mother is waiting for you there. She is lying down under a tree that in winter is as white as china, that in summer moves under singing birds. She has never known rest like this.'

I turned for home again, and as I cycled back I watched the far-off light in my window, at least I thought it was my window. The tyres reached the shallow water and sloshed through, so I dismounted and walked to where I had already checked twice for my brother. I let the bike down and before I knew it, fell on my side. No goggles. No matter, I lay with one eye under the water and one eye above. But I did not look because I was so comfortable lying down. Felt so heavy all of a sudden. The eye above the water watched the sun rise and the eye below stayed closed and the cold ran through me, chasing the sleep out of every corner and dark place, waking me up, wake Salt, wake up Salt, and the whole lake pushed at me with its chilly fingers, prodding me even though I felt more comfortable than in all my life before now, and all I wanted was sleep and I said thank you I am going to sleep now and I closed the eye above the water but the lake would not stop pushing me awake saying wake up, wake up, will you, I'm back, I'm here, wake up, I'm your mother, or it must have said wake up, brother, and this went on for a while and the day rose and light came into my eye again. Okay, I said. And I opened the eye below the water and finally saw him.

He was a couple of yards away, not much bigger than my hand and therefore I did not recognize the face though the shape had eyes, a nose, fingers, a mouth. He balanced himself in the currents, expert in the water, the only place he'd ever known. I wanted to move to him but could not. The arm pointed upward. I looked up at a pill shimmering on the water. He must have been warning me about the sky. What now – the sky – what was he warning me about? I gasped and rose through the surface and broke into the blazing sun.

The cold water sang through me and wrung me clear as a bell again, flushed out the pills. I knew it would not last, that the pills were lined up waiting for me at home, coughing and clearing their voiceboxes for the wailing, and I decided then and there it was time to get my father back and to have a chat with Fargoon.

I was back at the house before seven. First I found the pills in the bedroom and put them back in the fridge. I pulled off my raincoats and boots and socks and set the alarm clock for ten o'clock and covered the window with a blanket to keep the sun out because it pressed against the glass like a hand; and then I lay on my bed, wet and shivering. It seemed as if the pills yelled and sang and then screamed from the fridge, but I understood why and ignored them. I promised myself that I would ignore them for the day. I had three hours to sleep. It was early morning on Monday, December 21.

Before passing out, though, I gave my brother his name, the one I gave him twelve years before. He needed something to call himself as he was kind enough to offer to go to Pharmalak in my place. I agreed.

Because he had never seen the sun, I called him Sunless.

SALT 8

Sunless woke up and left the house at eleven this morning; he was gone for the day, gone to find my father. And he did – brought him back too, back for a decent burial.

When Sunless got home it was almost six o'clock, so I didn't have much time. I could see how exhausted he was and let him rest. I hadn't taken a pill all day and heard my head splitting its own bones, so I turned off the television in the living room and removed the blanket from my bedroom window, switched on all the lights in the house and lit a fire. I put the vase with my father's remains on the kitchen table. Back in my bedroom I opened the closet and picked up the envelope from a jacket I hadn't worn in two seasons. My name was on the cover, written in a hand other than the hand that wrote the notes. I brought the envelope to the kitchen and slit it open with a kitchen knife and pulled out a letter, two pages in blue ink, written on large sheets. The handwriting was careful but small. The letters slanted differently. My father's letter, written in the days before he died, which I could not bring myself to read in seven months.

I held the pages, one in each hand, though both shook so much I had to read and de-read each line several times. The first page detailed his finances, what he had in his bank accounts and a list of bills that had to be paid, elec-

tricity, water, a loan. I knew that my mother had paid those
bills, so he must have written the same things down for her.
The second page was for me.

I will be dead when you read this letter. I suppose I
shouldn't look back on my life: look what happened
to Lot's wife: a pillar of salt. Anyway, I hoped to
write more, a few letters, talking to you about how
you were as a child to help you put the pieces
together for the time ahead of you. I expected to
have a couple of weeks when I began writing to
everyone, and I was right; this last one has been
difficult to finish, as my hand shakes and the words
refuse to line up to where I want to put them.

As you know, I have donated my body to medical
science. There's not much left of it even as things are.
The Pharmalak facility will keep it for six months, and
when it is returned, you may dispose of it as you wish.

I have been shy my entire life, and you, Salt, were
the quietest boy. It's easily mistaken for arrogance,
and shy people know that more than anyone. If I
seemed distant to you when you were young, I
regret it and more so because a child cannot know
these things, though I also believe we don't give
children half enough credit for what they do know.
And now as you become a man, I am sorry again. I
don't want you to inherit my silence. You are old
enough now to befriend your mother. Please look
out for her and don't leave her on her own. I wish
you a happy and peaceful life.

Standing in the bright lights of the kitchen, I bowed my head and set the letter aside. I should have had the courage to read it right after he died. I didn't, afraid it would tear my insides out, which is what happened anyway by not reading it.

A man knocked on the door at 6.45 p.m. I had watched him come up the path to the house in the gathering wind.

I opened the door and he said, 'You're the person I'm taking to the cemetery? Pharmalak?'

'I'm here, ready,' I said.

He dropped his shoulder in deference. 'I'm sorry for your situation. Shall we go?'

He motioned me to the limousine waiting in the street, and I sat in the back seat. The car moved silently away and joined the highway.

'Weather coming,' he said.

'Yes,' I said.

To my left, the moon burned the edge of a snow cloud white to a breezy clear patch in the sky and the lake shone like tinfoil, with the moon so sharp that I could have turned it on its side and cut my finger on it. My body felt wide open and raw and the world rushed in, pumping everything to twice its size, twice as loud, twice its colour. If I wanted the world to go back to normal I would need those pills. Their pleading reached me from far away — amazing that I could hear them, that I could believe I did.

As we came to the cemetery on the west side of the city, the car turned right past the gate and on to a small road lined on each side with crosses and headstones until it pulled up to a space in the cemetery where a few men stood around a hole. I saw Jane also, dressed in a black coat. Behind them, a heap of clay, and at the edge of the grave, a coffin on a bier.

The driver left the limousine and joined the hospital chaplain, who stood with a scarf wrapped around his Bible. I did not want to get out of the car. It was big and clean, with the smell of polished leather. By night I could sleep in the back seat, and during the day I could watch the world go by outside. I could drive around for the rest of my life and never enter the world or my life.

But they were waiting for me. I walked up the slight incline to the graveside and stood at the head of the hole, where Jane nodded to me. I stared down into the hole, eight feet down, cleanly cut. The two gravediggers waited off to the side, leaning on their shovels; the chaplain came over and shook my hand.

'We should begin,' he said. 'It's rather late.'

I wanted to say something about whether it mattered that much to my father, as it had been rather late for him a lot recently. One of the clouds found the moon and swamped it. A deep shadow crossed the graveyard, moving across the headstones and reaching us, but the weak lights arranged around the hole kept everything visible. Sunless would have dived for cover.

'Then let's begin,' I said.

The chaplain motioned the two gravediggers.

We lifted my father's coffin, I on one side, the two gravediggers on the other, and it came up so easily, so easily we looked at each other without thinking. My father had been a good 180 pounds in life. Now the coffin was light enough to blow away in a good breeze, just some ashes and a few heavy objects to give the illusion of a body. We placed it at the edge of the hole. The chaplain unwrapped his Bible and read from it as another snow shower draped the field. Then the gravediggers handed me a rope and we lowered the coffin. When it reached the bottom of the grave, everyone stopped moving. They slowed down, I think, for me, to give me time, placing the ropes on the ground and standing aside. The one with the red cap tapped his pocket, as if looking for a cigarette. I looked into the hole at my father's remains. The breeze blew at the seconds.

And from that cloud, snow fell on to the pines of the cemetery.

My father's parts brought together for burial. I stood at the grave and wondered what a father was without a body. A memory, a collection of places and sounds. We were burying that and not much else.

I had not finished his letter to me. There was a third page, a passage he wrote that he asked me to read at his funeral, if he had one. I took the page from my pocket and said to the others,

'He wanted me to read this.'

The chaplain stood back. Jane tugged her cap from her ears.

I held the page to the swaying lamp.

'The ship. Not like the one we all made, your mother and I and you, to float on the lake. I'm seeing another ship. I spend so much time in bed these days, I see things and often wonder what's real and what is in my head. It's a wooden vessel with sails and a wide deck but only one sailor. It set out from shore the day I was born, first covering a huge bay with palm trees and then out into the ocean, day after day, moving toward me. Even in storms the sailor's hand held the wheel steady. Nothing stopped the ship, nothing pushed it back. It sailed the same distance on calm days and windy days, with one destination. It was coming for me, and the hour when it reached port was set the day of my birth. A few weeks ago I thought I heard the wood creaking, the sails blowing. But I know that when I do hear the ship, my ears will be shut of any noise. Yesterday I thought I saw the sails of this ship out on the lake. But I know that when I do see it, my eyes will be closed. I am not afraid. My son, goodbye.'

The snow blew away in a breeze and the night cleared to a patch of stars again. The chaplain and the gravediggers and Jane shone in the moonlight. I felt her hand on my shoulder. The world stopped for me, for a minute, and I didn't know what to think or say, so I thought and said nothing. The lamps moved our shadows around the head-stones. I tried to see the coffin, but it was too far down. My father's life with me and mine with him lay somewhere else, and now he lay under the ground, under my shoes, oblivious to me and the few people here, oblivious to the sky, to my mother, oblivious to the rest of my life.

He was gone.

I tried to feel something, but feeling was still some dis-tance away from my body. I shook the chaplain's hand, I shook Jane's hand, I shook the gravediggers' hands. Jane gave me her card and asked me to visit her and visit Fargoon, said the doctor would like that. When I reached the car, the driver was waiting with the door open for me. First I looked back. The chaplain and Jane had melted away on the other side of the grave. Already, the gravediggers shovelled their breath into the hole. I heard the first clay hit the coffin. I closed the door of the car. The driver turned the key and looked round to me.

'Well that's that,' he said. 'Home?'

'Home.' I spoke from my stomach, because the word 'home' meant little, a sound you made with your lips and tongue, a word that without substance manages to grind up your insides. But every sense had migrated to my stomach, a great flock moving across the empty grasslands, looking for water and a place to find rest and ease, propelled forward by some great unseen wisdom: that to survive you have to find a way to keep moving.

As the car eased down the road, I saw the diggers flash into the side mirrors, filling the hole where my father's body came to rest.

After the driver dropped me back at the house I went to the kitchen and sat in the dark. The feeling was back. Someone had taken a paring knife and gone through my hearing, my taste, my memory, my face, my worries, my hopes, my fingers, my eyesight, taken them and sliced them in strips and piled them one on the other across the floor of my stomach and said, 'Okay, Salt, now go and put yourself together again.'

I decided to go to bed with my clothes on, my boots and my coat, everything I wore to the cemetery. I opened the window, drew aside the blinds, stretched out on my back. It didn't take long for the cold to find the room: it poured in and, after covering the floor, rose steadily up the walls and filled the fibres of the mattress, and then made a blade against my skin, and then slid under it. But I should have felt colder, I wanted to feel the cold, wanted to shiver. That cold would not come. I thought of midnight funerals, Egyptian pyramids, the moonlight that drenched every dream I'd ever had.

The snow grew thicker, at least the flakes that fell to the light of my window. This must be what it's like to be dead. The blood stops and settles down. The organs sit in rows, wondering what to do now. I thought that sometimes cold was so cold it burned, and that's what really happened to my father's body up there in that hospital. He burned away coldly, lying with that formaldehyde in him, with his last expression on him. This must be what it's like to lose for real.

I was divided into parts too. A part of me hoped he wasn't gone, that he'd turn up one afternoon and tell me that he had, in fact, died but that it was all a mistake. He and I sit and talk for a while in the kitchen or at the edge of my bed, and he tells me what he can about what he felt and saw in all that darkness. I tell him everything I can think of, everything I failed to say to him even though I had all those years and all those words I knew to do it. I might even tell him the words sons have a hard time saying, that I loved him. That is, if I could, even after he was dead. And after I talk, before my eyes, he fades.

That's what happened: he burned away in my mind while I waited for him like a page when you strike a match to it. The brown rust advanced across the white page, and bit by bit, his body collapsed. The hands went, because they were at the edge of the page. The top of his head, scarred down to the forehead, then his face, all scorched.

Burn him all, I said. Never mind that hole. Take the body and burn it, burn it I say. And everything he left behind him. Why leave a splinter in the ground? Better a man go up in flames. Take him home in a handful of ash.

The snow was coming down: it whipped in off the lake, some of it driving sideways, a good two inches of it on the ground now. Nine o'clock. What to do? I brought the cup and saucer from my mother's room and placed them in the sink, shook the lemon wood polish and cleaned the table in the living room, vacuumed the carpet, and emptied the letterbox. And when that was done, I made toast and tea and brought them to the living room where I drew back the curtains and watched the silent storm.

Sunless would probably have something to say right about now. Soon he'd be back in the lake, stepping into the water that in a week or two would freeze for the rest of the winter. *Our father is in the ground.* What now, Sunless?

I know some more things, he says, walking into the kitchen and sitting at the table opposite me, and I go to the bathroom and throw him a towel and pour him some hot tea. I taste it first, invigorating, pulsing life into me. I construct the conversation with my lost brother.

'I know I have no grave,' he says. 'And I know that most people become invisible, they get lost in living, up for work, eat breakfast, read the paper, walk out the door, drive to work, work, return home, watch the television, go to bed, and every day they take up less space, and they don't see it happening to them. They lose sight of their friends too – it's easy not to notice people who do the same thing every day – and so slowly but surely the world recedes into the shadows year after year, and then one day you look for yourself and you can't find anything. You have become what the Greeks called a shade.'

I say I think I'm one of those too.

And one more thing, Sunless says. I have one more thing to say. Say goodbye properly, you coward. Go back and say goodbye properly. Do it. Do it now. You missed someone, didn't you?

I went to the bathroom, stood before the mirror and looked at what stood there looking at me. I pointed a finger at myself. *I accuse you.* And because it was a mirror, the other finger met mine at the tip, and I saw that the reverse was true. *You accuse me.* I poured water into the sink and bent to wash my face. The water dripped my face into the face of a stranger. I washed that face and pulled the plug and watched him swirl away. Then I took a towel and dried the face that remained, the face that must have been mine.

When I went back, Sunless was gone. Except he wasn't gone to the lake. I think I heard him start the car, and when I ran out, I saw tyre tracks in the snow, and I saw red lights disappear into the night, heading for the mountains, and the face of Sunless like a ghost's in the light of the instrument panel. I looked into the mirror again, but it wasn't the bathroom mirror. It was the rear-view mirror. I saw my own face.

I wondered if Fargoon was still at work this evening. If you are, Fargoon, you might want to go home, because Sunless is coming your way and he's brought a few questions with him, if I know Sunless.

THE KILLING OF MATTHEW
FARGOON

There are a number of things of which I am sure and a few
that are sketchy about what happened next over a period of
about one hour, after nine o'clock. Here they are:

Because he was driving his father's car, I am sure that
Sunless reached the foothills in under fifteen minutes. The
road crews were already out salting the highway and all the
lanes were clear, even when he veered left on to the creek
road and up the steep incline into the Wasatch range, heading back to Park City. He wasn't the only one driving up to
the resort town that Monday evening. Hordes of skiers had
heard the forecast the day before and had booked their
flights and flown in to the Lake City airport. In the morning they would fill the slopes around Park City, and some
would stay for Christmas. They came for their drug, and
only those who ski understand that the medicine is fed
through the eyes and nose and ears, the wide sweep of the
mountains under the blue sky and the hard white that let
you fly on the ground and fly in the sky at the same time.
It puts you between both worlds, like an angel.

But Sunless, I hear, had other things in mind. He drove
with a vase balanced on the dashboard because he wanted
to keep a good eye on it. If he placed it on the passenger

seat it might disappear. Things, Sunless noted, have a habit of disappearing in life if you don't keep a damn good eye on them and take care of them. People disappear too if you don't watch them. Sunless considered his father, for instance. One minute he's there and the next he's gone. And Sunless wondered about his mother; he couldn't find his mother. She must be hiding out in Florida, waiting for him to carry out his mission, his message, being an angel in reverse and getting her husband back from the high mountain castle where the bad Giant hid him. He wasn't about to let her down twice in one lifetime.

Sunless, and I am positive of this, reached the Pharmalak building at 9.49 p.m. and parked on the street. He brought the vase in with him and waved it at the lobby attendant, saying something about returning it now that it was empty and all and pointing upstairs along with checking his watch again. Because Sunless was dressed in a shirt and tie and jacket and good pants and shoes, the attendant waved him on. When the elevator doors slid open he turned left for Fargoon's office. The second floor was an echo because everyone had gone for the day, and the Pharmalak RX-24 health channel reverberated along the white, empty hall. He watched it as he approached Fargoon's office:

'A normal "difficult" child may have separation anxiety disorder, elective mutism, autism, attention-deficit hyperactivity disorder, and most common of all, a conduct disorder, which affects up to 16 per cent of boys and 9 per cent of girls. Have you talked to a doctor about your child's mental health?'

In the background, a flashing word, *Elevax*.

Sunless tried the door: the receptionist had not locked it behind her because she was used to working for a man who lived in his office. Yes, Sunless had evidently figured out Fargoon during their many talks over the months. This was a man without a family who worked into the night under his bulb in the slopes of a mountain ski resort, who most likely sipped a little light whisky after hours and watched the magic of Park City from his lonely little window. I can't be sure Sunless figured all that out, but Fargoon did have that whiff of loneliness about him. Anyone with a brain could pick it up.

Anyway, the story is that Sunless had some questions.

I presume Fargoon froze when Sunless floated into his office and put the vase on the table. His eyes may have darted to the door and to his telephone, but he may have elected to play it cool and to be the therapist, the good doctor, the president. I'll lay a wager he would have been better off running. One way he might have reacted was to lean back and say,

'You're back, Sunless.'

'I am.'

'Isn't it very late? Are the trains still running even?'

Sunless sat in his usual chair. 'I've been thinking.'

I'll bet Fargoon smiled. 'A dangerous pastime, I'm sure.'

'It's strange,' I believe Sunless said while bringing his fingertips together, 'that my father died because he didn't have health insurance. That was his disease, and it's a bit of a killer I hear. The strangeness of it is this, that he could have had his operation here if he had had the money, all he needed was a few doctors, a few hours—'

'This is not a healthy conversation.'

'He wasn't healthy when he died,' Sunless may have responded.

Fargoon doubtless said something like 'Yes, he could have been saved with an operation, though I doubt that your father's life could have been extended beyond a year in the best of circumstances – a difficult, painful, debilitating and dehumanizing year,' and counted each adjective with a finger. Sunless doubtless detected the fleck of sweat in the corner of Fargoon's right eyebrow as he continued,

'But he came up here and got all the doctors in the world to look into his disease. Look into it for months and months.'

Fargoon probably returned that lob with a swift forehand down the line: 'Your father asked us to treat him with an experimental procedure, to take his body upon death for science, asked us to put you on a drug trial so that you would have free health care, and requested that we also prescribe medicines for your mother, free of charge, all of which we were happy to do, admittedly predicated upon the donation of his body.'

Sunless, I think, admired how Fargoon didn't take any nonsense from him. Powerful men in large corporations can be surprisingly fragile: they'll snap like thin glass. Not this fellow. Fargoon was a wiry fighter whose life grew into medicine from persistence. He wasn't given anything by his parents.

'My father wasn't cured, my mother wasn't cured, and I wasn't cured.'

Fargoon definitely stood up at that moment: 'For

heaven's sake, man, no one is ever cured. They're temporarily stabilized,' and then he threw his hands into the air, a magnificent gesture, if he were standing in front of a big crowd in a market square or in front of legions or divisions of company representatives. Sunless most likely looked around him and saw only himself.

'Yes, but one person always gets sacrificed, and it was my dad's turn. What did you get out of him?'

In an objective report of the event Fargoon would have shaken his head and sighed, tried to open a folder but seemed too distracted to manage it. 'Your family fell through the cracks,' he said. 'Not poor enough for government health care, too poor for private health care. Millions like you, and I tried to help.'

'Did you extract the grief from him while it was still fresh inside him, for the pill? For Elevax? Did you get Elevax from my dad, I mean did his body help you make an antidote that led to Elevax?'

Fargoon apparently sat down and looked puzzled, even for a psychiatrist.

Sunless likely dipped his fingers into the vase and sprinkled some ash across Fargoon's desk.

'Here's my father now. There's his smile, there's his walk, there's his sense of humour, there's his disappointments, that's what he worked at, there is his memory of his own parents. And there's plenty more in here, all of him. The rest is falling from the sky.' And Sunless no doubt pointed to the window and the pitch-black mountain and if the doctor did follow, it was with his eyeballs only.

Something like this is what Fargoon said next: 'Did you go to the funeral?'

'Yes,' Sunless answered, and I know that he used that precise word. 'And while we're on the matter of the future, I wonder if I could get you to write down some more of my thoughts.'

Sunless may have come around the desk, or looked like he was going to, so Fargoon's standard line for that would have been, 'Of course, I think I can manage a very few short minutes.'

'I want to talk about the future instead.'

The rest of what occurred in Mr Fargoon's office is definite because it's all written down somewhere. Fargoon drew a line across the top of a page he picked from a pile in his drawer and wrote a word in capital letters and underlined that word then.

Sunless continued, 'I'd like to tell you about the future.'

'Your future?' Fargoon's fountain pen moved across the page.

'No, not my future.'

'Mine?'

'Not yours. I think the future is made up – what I mean is, the future doesn't exist.'

Fargoon sighed. 'Your thoughts on the future then.'

'Simple: the future isn't there. The chosen few make it up for the rest of us.'

Sunless paused to let Fargoon catch up. Outside, he was sure a light wind moved a big cloud across the valley because a flake hit the window and turned to water. But how would he know, he wondered. Only if it snowed properly.

He said, 'Ever been to your own future? I thought not. No future in my life, there never has been a future, there never will be a future, and it isn't in front of me. I can't move forward into the future, but I always hoped if it did exist it would be new, not made of bits of the past, a wife, husband, faces you've known. I've resigned myself to this: if there is one, it's more of the present.'

Sunless watched Fargoon's fountain pen scratch up to the last letter. He was getting good at reading upside down. When the pen stopped, he spoke again.

'The future is where you put all your hopes, and because it doesn't exist, you remain hopeless for the rest of your life. You hoped when you were a child, but today is where you have to live. The relief if you could ever say, "No tomorrow?" Good. And you can take the day after tomorrow as well. Tomorrow? I've never heard of tomorrow. When I go to sleep, I call that day "today". When I wake up, I call that day "today".'

Sunless stopped talking, not because Fargoon was catching up, but because Fargoon put the top back on his fountain pen and sat back in his chair, lightly touching his fingertips and arching his eyebrows.

'Take away the future and people have no reason to keep going,' the doctor said and looked at his watch.

Sorry, Vice-President of the Disorder of American Psychiatrists Committee Organization, Sunless knew that particular move, and said, 'Keep going where? How can you be worried about something that doesn't exist? That's what all pills must be for.'

Fargoon sat forward. 'Excuse me?'

'Pills, for worry about what isn't there.'

'Anxiety, Sunless.'

'Is it anxiety when you worry about what doesn't exist?'

'Yes.'

'That's why the future was invented, to avoid the present, but the future doesn't exist, and that's what causes anxiety.'

Fargoon nodded. 'Perhaps. But what has all this got to do with you?' He leaned back and joined his hands in front of his smile, obviously more comfortable now. That was fine, that was all right. Another gust of wind pressed the window pane.

Sunless looked out the window as he talked and Fargoon got back to writing. Dark, a few strollers, bundled up in jackets and earmuffs. 'How to make sure you never get anything: put it in the future. It's safer there than anywhere. *Tomorrow I will be happy*. I will be happy next year. And in the meantime, I have these pills. I hate my life. I hate my body. I am bored. I am lonely. I don't even like myself. In the meantime, I have these pills. In the future everything's going to be different. Oh really? I have news for you: no, it isn't going to be different, because there you'll be, standing right beside yourself.'

Fargoon shook his head. 'And that decision will not be made today. Not here, not today.'

Sunless agreed, said, 'Can we get some coffee? I've been up all day.'

'No. The receptionist is gone, and, in fact, the entire place is packing up for the holidays.'

Sunless fumbled in his pocket and then handed Fargoon a box of factory-sealed capsules he hadn't catapulted at people or swallowed himself. Good thing he didn't use all of them in the slingshot. Sunless then asked Fargoon to read him the information leaflet out loud, what it said.

Fargoon tipped his chair back. 'Nemocot is used to treat anxiety. This medication is thought to work by increasing the activity of the chemical serotonin in the brain. Anti-anxiety agent. Anti-depressant. Anti-obsessive agent. Anti-panic agent. Post-traumatic stress disorder agent. Social anxiety disorder agent.' Then he said, 'Sunless, this is in every single container for all drugs of its type.'

'Read the rest of that page,' Sunless said, and closed his eyes as if listening to a story.

'*Side Effects.* Drowsiness; trouble with thinking; problems with movement; fast or irregular heartbeat; fast talking or excited feelings or actions that are out of control; fever; inability to sit still; low blood sodium causing confusion, convulsions, dryness of mouth; lack of energy; serotonin syndrome (diarrhoea, fever, increased sweating, mood or behaviour changes, overactive reflexes, racing heartbeat, restlessness, shivering or shaking); unusual or sudden body or facial movements or postures.

'Other side effects that may occur usually do not require medical attention: decreased appetite or weight loss; headache; nausea; stomach cramps; tiredness or weakness; trembling or shaking; trouble sleeping; agita-tion; anxiety; blurred vision; constipation; increased appetite; vomiting. Other side effects not listed may occur in some patients.'

'That's it, that's that page,' Fargoon said and reached for a tissue and wiped his hand.

Sunless said, 'Isn't it strange that anxiety is a side effect of medication for anxiety?'

'Actually, no, it isn't strange at all. A perfectly normal response.'

'And why are they called 'side effects' and not 'effects'? Are they off to the side?'

Fargoon may have said nothing and attempted to stand, and Sunless probably let him stand and said, 'Other side effects not listed may occur in Sunless, for instance, investigations, photographs, tape recorders, sensors, spyware. Swallow this, Sunless, and you'll feel better. Sure. No wonder they call them "agents".'

Fargoon nodded and smiled, dropped his tissue into the waste basket under his desk and took a step as if absent-mindedly heading for his office door, but Sunless was ahead of him before he took a second step.

The rest is back to sketchy again. Here's my best guess.

Sunless said he had a headache and was shaking. He asked why Fargoon prescribed these drugs for his mother and for him. Fargoon said he hadn't, just for Sunless, that his mother was on the Xanax, that she'd asked for that and that he'd actually not prescribed anything, instead gave her a bunch of samples even though it was a restricted drug, to help the woman out. Gave her samples, Sunless said, and Fargoon said yes, that the Nemocot was for Sunless only, and Sunless agreed because he remembered opening a pack of Nemocot and putting one into the sling on the rooftop. But that left the matter of his mother.

'Your mother?' Fargoon said.

'Don't you bring my mother into this, did you ever hear me talk about my mother,' Sunless said and Fargoon shook his head and kept shaking it then. This is I think why: he wasn't doing it himself, and the reason is that Sunless was on top of him, meaning that he threw the rest of his father's ashes in Fargoon's face, the doctor spluttered and fell back in his chair and the chair fell back to the ground, and then Sunless was on top of him.

Afterwards, Sunless arranged some pills in a decorative fashion around Fargoon's office, meaning Fargoon himself, i.e., on him to be exact. A sprinkle of pills in his right and left eyes, a few along his lips, five or six stuffed into each ear, a small pile on his right breast, another on his left, pills on his right hand, pills on his left, and a few more in his pockets in case he ran out. Then a general throw of pills in the approximate area, to fall where they may. Now, since everyone was gone for the holidays, Fargoon would be here when they got back in a week or more, and he'd be foaming pills. Pills growing out of his face and legs and everywhere. They'd have to push in the door.

'Will you be all right?' he said to Fargoon and left.

It had to be about 10.35 p.m. when Sunless walked through the lobby and left the building. He strolled into Park City and went into a diner. The waitress placed a napkin and a cup of water in front of him, and Sunless positioned the empty vase directly between the knife and fork and ordered a soda. The waitress was nice – she smiled at him – he smiled back – she kept smiling – he looked down to his drink. I know it was hard for him to make that kind of eye contact, because my father once said he gave me that habit; he called it shyness, a condition that did its best to escape detection. Shyness makes you want to be invisible. You can carry it to extremes, but that's shyness for you. It makes you a tiny bit dead.

Sunless walked to his car about 11.15 p.m. The air was cool and quiet, with no sign of angels anywhere since his mission was completed, and the snow was snow again, since his father was completely emptied out of the vase and the sky now.

Sunless drove home and went back to the lake. I watched him go. It hadn't been much of a day in the sun for him. He left the knife with the blood on it with me.

An Angel Visits Emily Partridge

Actually, Sunless did make a detour on his way back to the lake. I know this because of what I heard later from the police, who shouted it through a megaphone at my house, and from other witnesses, who were awake that late when they should have been in bed. I've reconstructed the events from what I'm sure happened.

Sunless wasn't feeling that well at all because the pills were still in the refrigerator and were yelling louder than ever, asking him how he could stop like that after five months of taking them, that people can't do that and get away with it, but Sunless wasn't going to give in and open the fridge, not him. He was like that, always wanting to shoulder the world on his own: a hero without a pill.

After he left the house, he stopped by the house of the Partridge family, seeing as they were only a few doors down. They were all in bed, and Sunless didn't want to wake them so he let himself in through a side window Emily liked to leave open, which happened to be her bedroom window. He watched her asleep on the bed, her blonde hair spread like a stain in the moonlight; again, not wanting to wake her, he went off into another room for a few minutes and came back and started flapping his wings, and that's when she opened her eyes and screamed, but Sunless had closed the window and stood at the end of her bed. He raised and spread out the raincoat he was wearing with both hands.

'I'm here as an angel, so don't be scared,' he said.

'Yes,' she said.

'Now tell me the truth,' he said.

'Yes,' she said, sitting up, eyes right and left.

'Who said I was dragged off whose body? You said a body,' he said.

'Your mother. Her funeral last week. They let you out of jail and put you back afterwards.'

'Okay, because I thought you were there, at this funeral, the way you were talking when I came to the door the other day, if you recall by any chance.'

'No, I wasn't. Yes, I remember. I mean, I'm sorry.'

'You're sorry now, is that what you're telling me, Emily?'

She began to cry. 'I want my parents.'

'They're in the next room but they won't be coming in here, I asked them to stay there.'

Emily's hands covered her face.

'You know I got the fly in the end,' Sunless said. 'I destroyed the power structure of the entire organization with one blow of a plastic bag.'

Emily went under the covers and pretended to be a peanut, curved and motionless. Maybe he would not notice, forget she was there.

Sunless went over to her and flapped his wings until she flew with him around the room, and then he left the house and went to the lake. On the way the angel passed Mr Swan's house, saw him inside watching television, without giving him a second glance.

Back at my house, I wanted to take the pills so badly, they seemed to be rocking the fridge back and forth, singing 'Take us, take us.' They were going to wreck the house if this kept up. My head spun.

SUNLESS RETURNS

After the stop at the Partridge family residence, I think
Sunless stopped before he finally walked into the lake; he
stopped himself and came back. Something brought him
back. Maybe he wasn't ready to return to his tomb, maybe
he wanted to say goodbye properly: yes, that was it. He
came back to say goodbye properly, but not to me. And I
knew this. I knew what Sunless was thinking. He wanted
to say goodbye to his mother and father.

He was thinking about what happened to my mother.

That's what brought him back.

Some Observations from Sunless

My brother Salt was always too sensitive and lived out of a wound he carried with him everywhere, so that even walking was like bleeding, and if you said anything, which I never did anyway, he would probably defend his wound, holding it up like a shield if he depended on it for sympathy, or if he needed it for his identity, like a badge. And if you take the wound from some people, there's nothing left of them because they've constructed a whole new body around the wound and have let the other body drop away.

In my brother I saw what constant worry does to a face — what it does to all the faces in the world — how it brings out the demon or the angel inside. Some people wear their demon on their sleeves: they walk up to you and smile and shake your hand or ask you about yourself, and all you can do is watch the demon sitting on them like a hot insect on a green leaf in summertime. When he was young Salt carried an angel in him. He had a lightness in his worry. I wish he hadn't taken those pills, the ones our mother took. They carried demons in them that must have slipped in during the manufacturing and liked his bloodstream, and they sailed through his veins and into his heart, and then they crawled up to his eyes and looked out with black eyes, looked right at you.

I saw it happen. I think it was because of what happened to our mother.

My brother heard the jailer come to his cell door early in the afternoon. He heard the footsteps because the cellblock shackled everything down, even sound, and bounced it around the walls: men dreaming, men sweating, men thinking, all of it spread over the walls and echoing back at them, saying even your thoughts can't get out of this place, and saying again that you and your thoughts are stuck here, time is stuck here too, so you can stop counting the hours or the days. Time lives in months here. Count one month and try to forget time until another month is up. It's easier on you that way. Count the days and you'll end up as an echo yourself, you'll hear every second tick in your head and tick like another second and you'll say, wait, was that the second just gone or are you a new one, you see I need to keep count. But the seconds will crowd like a railroad station at rush hour and you'll be busy counting those seconds and they just won't stand still. They get into trains and glide off and new ones arrive on to the platform. And here's the thing: there are so many seconds and they count for so little. Like you. That's what the time of day will say back to you if you try to count it away.

The jailer opened Salt's cell. It was early in the afternoon, a Wednesday. Salt may have wondered why the officer stopped at his cell, and why his name was called by first name only as the cell door swung open and the officer pointed to him and said, 'We need you out here for a minute, Salt,' and a 'Not you' to his cellmate.

A sergeant waited in the hall and together they walked to the visiting room, where another police officer waited. It was explained to him that a neighbour, Mr Swan, had found a body in Salt's house. The coroner had been to the house and removed the body. Mr Swan had identified the body, and because he was a reliable witness, the coroner had accepted the identification. Not a crime scene, they said. The officer handed him a note. Salt looked at it, glazed over it, handed it back. The officer said they'd keep it for a couple of weeks and then return it. 'Why would I want that note?' Salt said.

The officer informed Salt that a judge had already signed a release order for one day, Friday, the day of the funeral, and then he had to return to finish the final week of his sentence. Was there anyone my brother wanted to call? Was there anyone my brother wanted to visit him in jail? As many visitors as he wanted. As many phone calls as he wanted. My brother shook his head as he went back to counting the seconds, but they were gone, all of them, and in their wake they left one second stretched on the floor, knives stuck in its flesh. He lost count of time. There's a look that creeps into the face when you've lost track of time, when you don't care. It's a blank expression in which every sense is turned off and turned on. It's the face of tree-shade on a hot day.

My brother did not believe in time any more because so many people he knew didn't have any time left.

On the Friday they drove him to a mortuary, and when he arrived, about twenty people stood around a coffin in the viewing room of the chapel. Some people shook his hand and said they were sorry. Someone flicked her head in his direction, 'prison, you know'. A man came up to him and asked if he would like to see his mother, since the coffin would have to be shut in a minute.

He walked to the middle of the room and stood at the coffin. She lay there, her eyes closed, skin drawn tight. The thin grey hair rested on the pillow, her shape bent in sleep like a broken coat hanger. He had never seen skin like that, bruised and drained at the same time, like a pile of grey rocks, and he wanted to look away but could not. Her hands, joined over her chest, looked like straws with bones inside them sharply outlined under the skin.

He remembered that hand one knuckle at a time.

The knuckle of her index finger. She trailed that finger along his forehead one day. He was very young, the youngest he'd ever been, so young he smelled her finger more than saw it.

Her second finger. He was older and lay in bed on a Saturday morning and she massaged his arms while she read a story. He could smell skin like honey and the fresh linen of the blue and white bedcovers. The sun came in the window but stayed in a corner where it heated the room without blinding them, like a piece of bright furniture.

Her third finger. She wrapped the wool around it when she knitted on winter evenings when he was six or seven years old: one in particular, a weekend his father read books while his mother made him a pair of gloves. He watched the needles crisscross and the single spool of string dart left and right, coming out the other side in a wall of red shaping into a hand.

'Magic,' he had said.

She liked that because she shook her head and smiled at the same time, and it looked to him as if her head were knitting something too.

He remembered the knuckle of her little finger when she

showed him photographs from when she was young. A picnic by a river long ago, young men and women at their ease on a sunny day. She explained who was in each black-and-white photograph, who was whose friend, and she pointed with fondness to one man: 'I was great friends with Mattie,' she said. There must have been feelings between them then. And as my brother thought about it, he wondered how many of them were alive after thirty years.

He did not know how long he stood there but soon enough the man moved at his side and touched his shoulder. Salt bent to kiss her forehead and stood back and tried to forget about all the people in the room as he said goodbye, and then wondered what goodbye meant, and he looked away for a second to gather himself, and at the moment the man moved the lid across his mother's face. He watched the shadow darken on her as the lid moved across and then covered her completely. And the man banged down the sides of the cover, six taps, all around the coffin.

Then his brother looked up at the faces of the living. Mr Swan, who found her, was the only one who returned his gaze. His brother remembered the cemetery and a hole in the ground and a box going into it. Grabbing at her coffin. People holding him back. The rest was haze. It was that kind of day, when seasons are switching places and the weather is uncertain, the sky elastic. Those are the days that can change your life.

Then they brought him back to prison to finish his sentence, another seven days, and he counted nothing of those particular days. They just passed him by and went on their way.

Mr Swan had told the police he hadn't seen her for four days and went by to knock at the door, though it was ten minutes before he had his hat and coat on, he said, and the police officer listened patiently, because Mr Swan talked as slowly as he walked and when he breathed in, you felt he was breathing in his next thought and had to wait for it to form into words before he could speak it. Yes, and after he knocked on the door and got no answer, he put his hand on it and pushed it open, and he called her name because he hadn't seen her leave, and when he wasn't watching television, Mr Swan spent a good deal of the day looking out the window in his armchair, and he hadn't seen her leave. When he didn't get an answer, Mr Swan told the police officer that he came up the hallway and tried the living room, the kitchen, and found her lying in the bedroom. The blanket was over her head, he said, and one of her arms lay on the blanket along with an empty bottle of wine and some pills.

During his final week in prison, Salt read his mother's note – late one night – the note with his name on it: 'Salt, I have taken some pills. It is already too late for me.'

And at that moment something in him swapped places with something else. Evidently he cannot say what it was or give it a name, but it knew his name, knew his body, knew where to go in him and to tell what had been there before to leave. He thought it might be an angel come to take over him now that he was defenceless.

After a week he was released. And the note was so heavy in his pocket that he had to put it away the minute he got back to the house. Couldn't have that lying around. It might be true.

But the pills were waiting for him. They were waiting. They knew their man.

But he did keep taking those pills, and although he stopped for a day he now had a few hours to go before the pills caught up with him. You don't get many chances in life to say goodbye, generally one if you're lucky. He had a few hours to be the old Salt again, the boy who lost his parents, to go back to where they lay and speak with them before the heavens came crashing down on him and the police sergeant drove at speed to Salt's house in the middle of the night in a flashing car along with other men in their cars and parked in a horseshoe around the empty house, stooped behind the doors and shouted through a megaphone for him to come out, to make it easy on himself.

People can't mind their own business. It's a law of the universe, written across the sky.

When the police came I was already at the shore observing the siege, and I could have stayed and watched, but the lake was cold, too cold to ignore, and I had no clothes. I walked up to my ankles – they froze and hurt, yes, I will admit that – but I walked on until the water reached my waist, and since it's a shallow lake I knew I could go no deeper, so I let myself fall forward and spread my arms wide like it was my first flight, and the lake grew warm around me and much smaller, and I heard again the voice of my mother though her skin when Salt put the page against it that he wrote, just for me, about breathing.

And above me, the pill floated briefly, and then the sky ate it.

The Year's Midnight

Back to the Cemetery

So Sunless was gone.

I had one concern returning to the cemetery: it was likely closed. I thought how that didn't make a lot of sense, closing time at a cemetery, and anyway, late at night seemed the best time to go, when the person living and the person dead were both in the dark.

I put the pills into my coat pocket and ran to my father's car and pushed the snow off the windshield with the kitchen broom, turned the key and coaxed the engine alive. Fumes crowded the back window, the heater blasted freezing air even though it had been driven shortly before, and the radio played an orchestra into the glow of the instrument panel that made my face a ghost's in the dark of the car. I reversed out the drive, reached the highway and headed east, speeding into the night with the lake to my left, under a break in the storm, a brief one this time, the clouds uncovering the moon and the moon the clouds, driving toward the yellow on the mountainside, Salt Lake City, gleaming with holiday decorations, the lights on the Christmas tree.

If Sunless were driving he'd have said that angels were falling from the sky over the graveyard. Tonight they weren't the only thing coming down. In the chaos of the windshield wipers I saw refrigerators, cribs, houses, snow, wind, syringes, pills, streets, pens, windows, notes, Fargoon, and more angels swirling and funnelling down over the stones in that field, images of childhood soaring and dipping, snapshots littering the sky above the cemetery, the snow forming faces and the wind tearing up those faces and driving them down to the ground.

I parked the car at the side of the road, approached the graveyard gate, and jumped the wall. Now to find her grave. The problem was that I didn't know where she was buried — on the day we buried her I was in a daze — and reading the headstones would be difficult now, even in moonlight.

I walked the small path to my father's plot. The gravediggers had patted down the clay and placed a temporary stone with his name and a wreath, no doubt from the hospital. I sat on the grass for a minute and looked around at the stones and monuments that drew neat lines down the slope to the road to the city.

Taking a few pages of the notes Fargoon made in our sessions, I held them face down to his grave. Can you read these? This is the person I became after you, how much I miss you. Could you have been friends with a man who said these things?

I checked the graves on each side. But I did not recognize the names, and I wondered if my father had ever passed the strangers in life he would be buried beside. Walking further to the right, I moved along grave after grave, passing by any that looked older than a few months. Most were. When I reached the wall, I turned and moved back along a different line of graves. Back at my father's, I moved left this time, reading off the names as I went. Soon I was able to glance at a stone and know that more than a month had passed since a burial, and I started to read the dates instead: the nineteen hundreds, a couple from the eighteen hundreds. At the cemetery wall I moved to the next row and walked back along that one. Some of these people had been quite important in life, or quite loved, judging by the size of the headstones. And some not.

I did this for twenty minutes, walking along line after line of headstones, graves, monuments, flowerbeds, statues. I passed under drooping trees, past the lines people wrote promising that they would meet again, lines that tried to say what was written elsewhere and unsaid.

What an interesting position to be in, to be lost among the dead. I smiled and I didn't know why. A conversation with a stranger in the cemetery might go like this: 'I've lost my mother. I did the same with my father, but I've found him. Yes, I've found my father and I'm looking for my mother. No, I don't need any help, but thank you all the same. Sunless told me to say goodbye properly and I thought he was talking about my father, but I think he meant both.'

Someone, it occurred to me, should live in a cabin in the cemetery, or at least overlooking it, someone who lives in candlelight so that you can see his shadow and knock on his door if you need directions, that is if he doesn't see you first and come to help. He is a keeper of graves. Perhaps he is employed not only to live among the dead but to know the history of each person buried in the cemetery, to remember those he never knew. And when schoolchildren come to visit out of yellow school buses, as on visits to a museum, he brings them to a grave and says, 'Here is Johnny Armstrong, who died in 1986. Let me tell you about where he grew up and who his first friends were.'

And even if the keeper of graves were the best storyteller with the best memory, the schoolchildren might still assemble in their imaginations an imperfect recollection of this invisible Johnny Armstrong. Why were the dead buried anyway? The earliest graves, dolmens and pyramids, rose above ground. Below ground the dead were doubly invisible – that is, buried in coffins and those coffins themselves buried out of sight under a stone with a name carved into it. Stone, the most durable of substances, represents flesh, the first to rot. Because stone remains forever, how long should a body stay in a graveyard? Until family and friends are gone and no one visits any more? After that, why keep a grave?

Someone at my mother's funeral said I would see her again, see my father too, one day. I think I may have said something back, a question that if I did see them, what age would they be? When they were young, in their twenties, or when they got married, or will my father look like he did when he was sick and my mother when she was with her friends by that river thirty years ago?

My head cleared up: maybe it was the weather blowing away the pills.

As I walked the lines of stones, I wondered how much more a child could know of a mother and father; my parents' friends may have known them as much as I did, and more. Maybe companionship is the great reward. The Arabs say that at a certain age a son becomes a brother to his father. I did not reach that age in time. Another few years and we could have been friends.

I lost so many friends when I was young, but the hurt soon faded, an echo of what I felt for them. If you felt much love, the grief will weigh the same. And if you loved someone all of your life, the grief will live inside you always, because your body is the only body big enough where it can live. And it can pass through generations, like the viruses in the hall of cylinders. A mother's loss is passed on to a daughter over twenty years of thinking. A boy feels the pain of his father's father, whom he never knew, or about whom his father never says nor has ever said a single word. But people found the courage to go on. Time passed or something new was born in them, and they managed to go on with life, to go forward. I caught myself saying that, going forward. The future was still out of the question, no room for the future, no vacancies, come back another day, when the future isn't just more of this feeling.

The more I walked along the headstones, the more I wondered if I would find her at all. My search would be far easier if the graves were organized according to some principle other than date of death. Some part of me said that, though all the rest of me dreaded the moment I found her.

Perhaps they could reserve sections for men, for women, for boys and girls; or perhaps by profession – for lawyers, for professors, for truck drivers; perhaps by inclination – for the depressed, the joyful, the optimists, the pessimists, the jealous, the spiteful, the wistful, the remorseful, the stoics; perhaps by the number of friends a person had – those with many friends placed closer to the road and thus more accessible, those with fewer, off into the middle of the cemetery, where few would come looking for them anyway and where their privacy could continue into death; and perhaps a section could be reserved for suicides – or they could be kept out altogether, buried instead at cross-roads. If so, the rule makers would have a hard time distinguishing between the suicides who took their lives in a moment of despair and those who did it over years or decades, by remaining in marriages, smoking cigarettes, or by being angry all the time.

If you buried people according to their profession, though, you'd probably hear things like, 'I don't want to die a salesman, I mean I don't want to be a salesman when I die' – 'I don't want to die a media consultant, I don't want to be buried as a consultant.' And if people were buried where they lived, you might have people realizing long before their death that they did not want to lie for ever in Maryland or Florida or the Upper Peninsula of Michigan. So they'd move and start new in a better place for them.

Best of all, create a city of the dead. You can walk the corridors of this city, the alleys, the parks, and find your departed above ground. You can drink coffee and shop for bread with the dead stacked everywhere around you. I had read once where monks in Ireland slept each night in their coffins.

What, I wondered, if I could know the date of my own death from the moment of my birth. What if I lived life backwards, knowing the time of my death but not when or where I was born and under what circumstances, and my entire life was spent working toward that moment of my birth, wondering about my origins, not my destination. Would I live life any better?

I came to a stretch of new graves, and, of course, the moon went under a cloud and I had to bend close to the stones to read them, even running my fingers along the carved names.

And before I wanted to, I came to my mother.

MOTHER

Her grave had a small headstone because it takes months for clay to settle before they put the final, heavy gravestone in. She was buried down the slope, her grave next to a large mausoleum with two stone angels placed on pedestals to either side of the door. I walked past the mausoleum and stopped at the angels. They both held swords, their stone faces looked down to the ground, stone faces from which the sculptor had wiped all emotion – no pity, no resolution, no justice, no joy, no friendship, no personality, no name, no recognition, no loyalty – and I closed my eyes and felt how cold these messengers really were, remembered them towering over my mother's small grave when we buried her, that's right, those huge angels at the mausoleum of what must have been an important person. I opened my eyes and looked at their faces again. All the humanity gone, and then I recognized that something had been left in those faces by accident or design: what survived the chisel, or what the sculptor placed there, covering their wings, their stone eyes, loosening the hands that held the swords as if they were dropping them, was compassion.

Another few steps and I found her. It was strange to locate my mother by her name, her whole life stripped down to those two words on a plain, small headstone in the moonlight. My father lay a hundred yards away. Strange that he had died six months before her but was buried after her.

I thought of the bed of the lake and the snow falling on to the salt. A few flakes touched my hands as I stood there, sticking my skin with cold dots, stitching a white skin on top of my own. I didn't know if it were true that no two flakes are the same, that each has a pattern like a web. What I knew was that this real cold came from nowhere and everywhere at once, and for the first time in a long time I felt it. I didn't know where the wet on my face came from, but when I my put my fingers on my cheeks, the wet was there, and when I tasted it, it was salt. I dabbed my fingertip and held it out in front of me. Such a large amount of grief in a small amount of salt.

My mother's body: the only body I ever came from, the other body I lived inside. And now I wanted to go back if only for the second and last time. So I wrapped my coat around me and lay down on her grave, directly above her. I lay face up and imagined her lying under me. She was most likely lying on her back. I watched the clouds race light across the night and across the cemetery. Of course, no one in this graveyard felt the cold that the wind blew, and neither could I, so I stood, removed my coat, my shirt, my pants, stripped naked, and lay again on her grave. I closed my eyes and waited to feel something. Now everyone in the graveyard stretched perfectly still, and the only evidence anyone would have that I was alive would be my heart and my breath, and those only if he approached. Some minutes passed, but I tried not to feel those minutes because no one else here felt them. I wondered how long

I could last like this, lying in my bare skin: five minutes multiplied by a hundred and then a thousand fives? The ice took hold of me, lifted me in its hands, shook me.

I listened for the sound of clouds, of grass, and after a while, I stopped listening for anything.

What I felt was comfort, lying with my mother, as I did when I was a child and she kept me close to her when she slept. The cold shook my body and said, 'You are the one who's alive.' So I put my coat on top of me like a blanket and turned face down. When I opened my eyes, the moon had moved.

I warmed the clay and snow that pressed back at my face and denied my entrance to the underworld. But the underworld was eight feet away. Eight feet from the body that produced mine from inside it. I closed my eyes fully and made claws of my hands, scraping the earth until it tore away to harder clay and small stones. When the clay filled my hands I knew I could go further, and I dug faster, lying face down under my coat. At a certain point I could go head and shoulder first, dig wide enough to make it down to her coffin by crawling.

When I reached the wood I could take a stone and batter it open. It's dark down there and the moon is hidden behind my body, but splinters of light cut into the coffin, and I see her face. I came from that body. And I lie on top of her, and when that isn't enough, when I know that I must go inside her to find that place I lived for the first time, I enter her by thinking and sinking as only happens in a dream of what's possible. I move aside her skin and find her lungs, move them aside and see her womb. Did I come from here? And where in all of this is my mother now? And

I lie on her and try to warm her. Then I take her heart, still beating, in my hands and hold it to my face, hold it there and feel it beating. And I say to the beating heart, 'Mother, are you there?'

Lying naked, face down, eight feet above her, I thought of holding a trial. By searching carefully inside her body, I could find the pills that killed her and line them up. 'Which one of you killed my mother?' Two suspects step forward, Secanol and Lorazepam. They testify, as they have no choice, since I've caught them red-handed inside her. The coroner chased them through a phial of her blood and in less than a day found them hiding. One says, 'She took a handful, a number of us, and I gradually suppressed her heart beat. The wine helped me do my job. Another, Elixir of Aprobarbital, steps forward out of her body. 'So did I. But we were only instruments.'

I heard them speaking from under the clay, holding forth in her coffin.

Then I could move the trial up the slope at my father's grave, to find and prosecute the pills in my dad. 'Which one of you failed to save him?' And one by one they step forward and give their names, long chemical names: 'My name is Atenolol and I failed to save your father.' 'My name is Nisoldipine and I could have helped but could not because of him. And it points to another, which moves forward and says, 'Yes, I counteracted the previous medicine, but that is hardly my fault. That is the doctor's fault. What this man needed was an operation.'

Then a fourth and fifth medicine step forward, one hiding behind the other. 'Yes, we failed in tandem, though I was the lead medicine and the one behind me ancillary, to relieve the pain.' And Phenobarbital says, 'He could have ended it all sooner if he had taken a certain amount of me, but he did not. Your father was a strong man. We were there, lying in a bottle, all he had to do was take us out and pour us into his palm and lift his palm and open his mouth and swallow with some water, but he did not.'

And the inhaler steps forward, still encased in its pumping mechanism, the one that still has some medicine left in it, and it says, 'I helped your father breathe, but that was my sole function. I did not reverse his disease. What I did was keep him alive longer, and in a sense, therefore, I prolonged his suffering.' The judge at that point says, 'I must ask you not to use the word "therefore", as it is an extremely traitorous word.' 'Very well,' the inhaler says, 'I collaborated with the others but I think I did the least damage. Without me, he would have died sooner and suffered less. I was an instrument of delay, until he ceased breathing, that is, and then he did not take me up any more and I was gathered with his other medicines and put into a bag.'

My father's stone was somewhere up the slope among a hundred people — he was in there somewhere. Even in death, I was talking to him at a distance. I reached for the pillbox in my coat and opened it and threw the pills as hard as I could over the graves. Some landed on headstones, some on flowers. 'Take these and you'll all feel better,' I shouted. No one emerged to take the pills. At that moment I felt the chill and looked at my hands and my arms, and yes, I felt the cold, the real frozen midnight, everywhere on me. Snow fell on to my arms, on to my head, my shoulders, the skin of my back. I put my hand on her headstone.

It was the shortest day of the year, the year's midnight, and I left my hand on that stone until I felt my own bones. The moon appeared between clouds, so bright I thought I could see my bones too. Yes, I may have seen my bones.

'I will be alive,' I said, 'when I wake tomorrow. Tomorrow. I can see the future again.'

But Sunless, my brother, he needed rest. He must have been tired growing up with me, without a body, always having to follow me and live with my dreams, belonging nowhere for himself. He had one day in the sun: that was his lot. And that was what he pointed to this morning, to the sun. But he was pointing it out for me. I closed my eyes and opened the door to the dark he lived in and let him go.

There was an agony coming and no one could help me now, so I decided to postpone tomorrow and join my brother soon in the lake, put my head under the water and call for him again.

Standing in the falling snow, I looked down at her grave. I wasn't sure what was inside me. Along with the ice in the air, I felt a heat that I thought might be my father or mother or both, as if they were back again after an absence, or perhaps they were inside me for the first time, since they were gone for ever now as well; and maybe because of that feeling I was able to drape my coat and shirt and pants across the clay to warm her, letting the flakes cover me, and I said to her that life was cold too, and not to worry about me, that things would be better from this moment on, and anyway, that she was resting.

I'm sorry I left you alone. I miss you more than I can say.

I looked up from my mother's grave and down into the sky, and then down more, down into the stars.

ACKNOWLEDGEMENTS

I want to express thanks to my agent Sarah Chalfant and to my editor Ben Ball for their invaluable help, and to Christina for her reading, and to Natalie for her reading and for her desk in the corner.